Emergency Lullabies

Also by
Feathers

Emergency Lullabies

MADELINE NIXON

This is a work of fiction. All names, characters, businesses, places, events, and incidents are either the products of the author's imagination or used fictitiously. Any resemblance to actual person, living or dead, events, or locales is purely coincidental.

No part of this book may be reproduced in any form or by any means without the written permission of the Author, except by reviewers who may quote brief passages in reviews.

Copyright © 2023 Madeline Nixon
All rights reserved.

Cover Design by Clover Akuoko-Dabunkah and Anjelica Maglinao
Designed by Madeline Nixon

ISBN-13 (print): 978-1-7389907-0-2
ISBN-13 (ebook): 978-1-7389907-1-9

To Riley and Sophie,
you are my Poppy

Chapter One

The last time I had to run track was in grade nine gym class. Eleven years ago. I have not intentionally been running since. I have especially not intentionally gone running in a red string bikini that provides absolutely zero boob support and gets you side eye from all the chic summer moms the second you step out of your pastel yellow VW Bug and onto the spongy playground turf.

In hindsight, not my best idea.

In hindsight, I probably should have known I'd spend my time at the splash park chasing after Poppy. At nearly two (or as the moms congregated under the gazebo and on the benches at the park say, twenty months old), Poppy has mastered the art of running. And God help me because she is so much faster than I am.

I made a mistake. Because running after a dainty toddler who has no business being as fast as Donovan Bailey is no joke. (My dad will tell you at any given opportunity that he went to high school with him. For one year. Three grades apart.) And running after said fast little gremlin in a top that makes every part of your upper body jiggle is even worse.

"Poppy!" I shout, pretending I'm not out of breath and incapable of keeping up with a child whose legs are less than half the size of my own. "Poppy, don't you want to go down a slide? Or we can go under the elephant's trunk together!"

I came to this damn park on the hottest day of the year solely because of that elephant and the bucket of water it dumps out its trunk. Poppy is too preoccupied, though. The kid's a runner and the sidewalk surrounding the park is a racetrack. I pause and follow her with my eyes, mapping the best way through the park to snatch her up, but in those five seconds of pause, I see what's going to happen.

"Poppy!" I shriek through a sudden arc of water from a fountain two inches to my left.

Poppy puts on the breaks a moment too late and crashes into the legs of a tall bearded man with a water gun slung over one of his broad shoulders. She bounces back, falling on her diaper-cushioned bottom, but not before reaching for something to break her fall. She finds purchase on the crocheted dress of the little girl standing next to the man. I stand frozen in shock as the little girl, obviously not expecting a sharp tug on her dress, crashes down beside Poppy.

"Fucking hell, Pops," I whisper to myself as I jog over to her side of the park.

Her screechy cries greet me as I walk up and gather her into my arms. Her face has crumbled from its usual mischievous smirk and confident bright eyes, her nose and cheeks now red from the force of her crying.

"You're okay, Pops," I say, stroking her sunshine hair.

"Just took a little spill. You're all good. A bruised butt and ego, that's all."

Of course, she's a baby and she scared herself, so my words do little in the moment, but I still hold her close to my chest. As I comfort her, I realize there are eyes on me and curse myself for having such terrible mom instincts, even though I'm not a mom. I'm an aunt. Or a nanny. Or something. But a mom would have immediately apologized to the man and his child, right?

"I'm so sorry," I say as Poppy's sobs lessen against me. I have about a minute before she tells me she wants to go home, her general response after injury and embarrassment.

"Don't worry about it," the man says and gestures to his daughter, who has already shrugged off the accident and run into the park. "Like you said, it's just a spill. No harm done."

I sigh and turn back to him, meeting his ice-coloured eyes. "Oh," I say. I know him. The beard and kid are new, but those eyes . . . him. I've known him since grade seven. "Theo."

Shock registers on his face and he tilts his head, as if trying to place me. I can't help but think he might be wondering whether we've slept together. Which we haven't. But the rumours in high school around him and the hockey team made it seem like they had a new piece of ass every weekend.

"Magnolia," I say. And if that isn't enough, I add, "Magnolia Callas. We went to high school together."

His eyes widen slightly, and a smile spreads across his face. "I'm sorry, I didn't recognize you. Your hair is so plain now." I subconsciously run my hand along the blonde ponytail snaking down my back. "I don't remember you ever having the same colour in your hair for more than a month. I think it was purple at graduation."

"This is my natural colour," I say, not quite meeting his eyes, not quite comfortable with a confrontation of my past self and the fact that I haven't dyed my hair since Poppy was born.

"I like it," he says. "It suits you."

"Home," Poppy says into my neck.

I pull her tear-stained face away from my body and smile at her. She sets her features into a pout, crossing her stubborn, pudgy little arms. I clock the odds of a massive temper tantrum if I run through the water with her, then decide to do it anyway because this heat and this meeting is too much for my sweaty brain.

"She's going to hate me for this," I say, half to myself and half to Theo. He chuckles, clearly familiar with this particular thought process.

"Do it," he says as he strips off his shirt. I try to avert my eyes, but I can't help but notice the sculpted planes of his chest. He's still in great shape. "There's only so long you can run around a splash park as an adult without it looking weird."

I smirk. He shifts and pulls the water gun from his shoulder, then zeroes in on his daughter.

"Good luck," I say and giggle as he salutes me.

"Good to see you again!"

Theo runs off toward a large fountain and fills up the gun. The summer moms eye him appreciatively and eye me with a hint of disdain. I roll my eyes and ask Poppy if she's ready. She nods enthusiastically, curls bouncing. And then she screams while I cool us down running underneath the spray of water from a metal elephant's trunk.

Chapter Two

I sit in the Bug outside the townhouse I could never afford, willing myself to be happy for my best friend. I am happy for her. Hanna deserves the world and more. But I still mourn the life I once lived and the track I once was on. Hanna's new house is a reminder of that.

The clock on the dashboard ticks away another minute. I'm officially twenty minutes late to our unofficial housewarming. I kill the engine, then pull down the driver's side visor. Despite feeling like I could cry, again, my mascara is still pristine on my eyelashes. I snap the visor back into place and open my door in one fluid motion. I slam the door and round the car to grab my housewarming present from the passenger side. One specific and possibly underrated talent of mine is my ability to put together solid-looking gift baskets containing items from Dollarama. A blanket, a candle, brownie mix, fake flowers and a vase, two wine glasses, and mugs filled with hot chocolate all thrown in a cute little basket show I made the effort without spending an exorbitant amount of money. It also looks cute as hell.

And then there's the wine I brought, which shows that

I like wine and would like to spend this night drunk and avoiding the fact that my life is eons behind Hanna's.

   I lean against the car and stare up at the house. Hanna and Drew got lucky. After losing countless bidding wars on houses they claimed were their dream homes, they finally found the right combination of place and price in this little house a half hour outside our hometown. Each house in the line has its own character, different colours and front facades. Hanna and Drew's has deep-red brick, with stonework around their single garage and doorway. A staircase that could rival homes in Montreal leads up to their front door, gingerbread-like arches peaking below their dark shingles. It's such a cute starter home, not unlike the one my sister, Iris, and her ex-boyfriend almost bought.

   With a sigh, I push myself into a standing position and make my way up the stairs. Hanna opens the door on the first knock, almost as if she was waiting for me. And she probably was. She looks perfect, as per usual, her tawny brown skin glowy and curls framing her face like a halo.

   "These stairs are like an Olympic event," I say.

   She laughs that big, open laugh of hers. "I know. They're my workout, but killer after a night shift."

   "Bless you," I say as I hand over the wine. She leads me back into the kitchen, a cozy and warm room, with light wooden cabinets and speckled blue countertops. I plop the housewarming basket down next to the wine. "Where's Drew tonight?"

   "He's at his mom's place. She broke her ankle last week, so he and his sister have been taking turns helping her out," Hanna says with a shrug. She reaches for the plastic wine glass with a gold rim from my basket and smiles appreciatively. "Besides, it's girls' night, so I don't mind him not being around."

I laugh and accept the glass of white wine. I bring the glass to my lips and take in her new house. Tears prickle at my eyes, but I blink them away. Wine may or may not be a good idea tonight. I drink.

"So, tour time?" I ask.

Half an hour later, Hanna and I laze on the sectional couch in her family room. Some fall Hallmark movie plays in the background. We've refilled our glasses. The bottle I brought sits next to a bottle of rosé on the coffee table.

"No one tells you how much energy wedding planning takes," Hanna moans.

"I think everyone tells you that. But also, isn't your wedding date like, two years away?"

"Yes. Don't judge me. And okay, maybe they do tell you how much planning it takes, but no one ever tells you how shit it is when you're working and in school at the same time, and trying to find a house."

"Well, now that's just too specific," I say with a smirk. "How's that going, by the way?"

After the worst of the pandemic, Hanna nearly quit her job. Working as an Intensive Care Unit nurse, as one would expect, had been incredibly draining. Instead, she pivoted, applying to and starting a nurse midwife program in the fall of 2022. Her second year starts next week.

"I've loved it," she says, wistfully twirling a coil of hair around her fingers. "You know I would never willingly take a summer course for something I didn't love."

I laugh. I remember her hatred from the one time

she took a pathophysiology summer course during her undergrad. The professor was a mess and, with a condensed timeline, the course was like information overload. She never took one again until now. Which I guess says a lot about how much she's fallen into the best place she could be in life.

And how much I haven't.

"Hey, it's your song!"

I choke on my last drip of wine. Sure enough, in the background of the Hallmark movie is the song I sold when I was nineteen. My one and only accomplishment in life. I'd thought that meant something back then—that I'd easily sell more from there and become the singer-songwriter my sister and I had always dreamed of. But life had other plans.

I clear my throat and sit up to pour more wine into my glass. "So, I ran into Theo today."

"Hennessy?" Hanna screeches.

Like almost every girl at our Catholic high school, Hanna had the biggest crush on Theo. That is, until he wrecked my culminating project in grade eleven and we both decided his good looks weren't worth his behaviour.

"The very same," I say and down the glass I've just poured. "You know, I kind of hated his guts after what he did, but I also kind of miss the hockey bros yelling 'Hennessy' down the hall."

"Hennessyyyy!" Hanna imitates and giggles. "Yo HenAssy!"

We break down into wine-induced and nostalgia-fuelled laughing fits. I pour from the bottle of rosé and settle back into the couch, drawing my legs to my chest.

"Okay, but get this. Hennessy has a kid."

"No fucking way!" she yells. "I mean, I guess I believe it. He fucked everything that walked, and I guess that kind of catches up with you eventually, but he's a dad?"

"He's a daddy."

Hanna snorts and covers her mouth with her hand. "So you met a DILF at the park. Good job, Lia."

"I didn't meet a DILF, I met Theo Hennessy. Big difference."

"So how old is the kid? What do they look like?"

"If I had to guess, I'd say she's six or seven. And I didn't get a great look at her cause she ran off pretty fast, but she has, like, brownish red hair like him."

Hanna pauses for a moment and counts on her fingers. "Did he have this kid straight out of high school? Why do we not already know about this?"

"His Instagram is private. Probably because of the kid. And we don't really hang around with anyone who hung out with him, so . . ."

"I cannot believe he's a dad."

"I cannot believe he's a good dad."

"Oh, that's hot," Hanna says. "Get me a guy that's a Mr. Mom."

I laugh. "Dude, you have Drew. I'm pretty sure he's out Mr. Momming his mom right now."

She smirks and raises her glass. "Cheers to that!"

I lie on my back on Hanna's couch, staring up at the ceiling as she snores lightly. Her dark mane of hair falls in tangled webs over her face. It's a sleepover like old times where we both passed out on each other's couches, whether as little kids or big kids in university dorms. The only difference is that this time I can't sleep and the wine stirs questions in my mind.

I've long since put down my phone. It only furthered my anxiety once I saw a specific Instagram post. A friend I went to school with before I dropped out of the program got her dream role in a Broadway show. I liked the post in the darkness of Hanna's family room, then threw my phone onto the couch.

I was meant to do something with my life, and I let it go. Maura and I were top in our class at the Glenn Gould School, The Royal Conservatory of Music. Now she's the first Asian Canadian Glinda on Broadway and I am here, trying not to cry on my best friend's couch.

My sister died the day before the Holiday Showcase. I didn't go back. I went to Europe instead.

And now I'm an unpaid nanny for her child by day and a bartender by night. To say that my life is a far cry from where I thought it would be is an understatement.

Chapter Three

Drunk and depressed me impulsively bought tickets to The Wiggles last night. After hours of staring at Hanna's popcorn ceiling, I finally fell asleep, only to wake up a few hours later when my phone rang. My mom got a notification about the concert as I'd apparently used her email to confirm the tickets and wondered when I was coming to get Poppy.

I run a hand over my tired eyes as I search for a parking spot. Excitable kids and their similarly tired-looking parents scamper between cars. I narrowly avoid hitting a rogue child and refrain from slamming on my horn lest I scar them for life. But I do swear like a soldier, then cover my mouth, hoping Poppy heard none of that.

A giggle comes from the back seat, then, "Fuck," in a tiny voice.

"Poppy, I love you, but no," I say.

She continues her fit of giggles, because all children take great joy in repeating your mistakes. I can't help but smile, even though the other part of me is praying she never repeats that around my parents. I know she probably will. It's not the first time I taught her a swear word. But at least *shit* isn't as bad as *fuck*.

Finally, I pull into a spot, wedging the Bug between two minivans. I heave a long sigh. Here we go. First time at a concert in three years and first time back in a theatre since Iris died.

I plaster a smile on my face as I open the back door and greet Poppy in her pink car seat. She kicks her legs, joyfully. Mom dressed her in a bright-yellow T-shirt and a white tutu with a black skirt overtop in an attempt to make her look like Poppy's favourite former Wiggle, Emma. My hasty scanning of the parking lot tells me that almost every other parent of a daughter has had the same idea.

"Ready to go party, Pops?" I ask her. She squeals her assent.

I gather her into my arms, not trusting her to stay by my side as we make our long walk to the theatre. I push my bag up on my shoulder, then nudge the car door shut with my hip.

"Are we going to go see The Wiggles, Poppy Girl?" I ask, getting her that much more hyped up. "We're going to dance with Anthony, and Simon, and Lachy, and Tsehay, and Lucia, and John? And we can't forget about Wags the Dog! He's your favourite, isn't he?"

"Doggy! Doggy!" Poppy says with her grabby hands reaching out toward The Wiggles posters lining the outside of the theatre.

"We'll have to see if they have a Wags doll, won't we?"

Poppy grins and babbles as I push through the doors to the theatre. I'm not sure I've ever seen this many children together at one time outside of a school. Everywhere you look, children are dressed in blue, red, purple, and yellow, professing their allegiance to various Wiggles.

"Miss!" a man in an usher's uniform calls to me.

I jump and realize I'm blocking the doors. I hand him my ticket with a flourish. Kids under two don't need their own ticket, which may or may not have been a reason I splurged on one singular ticket to The Wiggles a day before the concert. The going rate for these things makes it seem like they're Adele or something. Though I guess to kids, they are.

Once my ticket scans, I walk farther into the venue, absently telling Poppy everything I see. I point out all the children dressed up like her and she claps gleefully. I find the merchandise tables, set up in front of what would usually be the bar. Among dolls of each Wiggle, glow sticks, sippy cups, and more varieties of shirts than I've ever seen at an adult concert, sits Wags the Dog. The plush is fun-sized, just like my little Poppy, with its tongue sticking out and a brown *W* embroidered on its stomach. I pick it up, show it to Poppy, then take it over to someone working the booth.

Poppy melds with the plush. She holds it to her chest, and I fully believe she will never let it go. I readjust her on my hip and head toward the auditorium, ready to put down twenty pounds of child.

I guess I hadn't thought about how this would feel when I bought the tickets at 3:00 a.m., but now . . . I don't want to go in. I don't want to be in the audience when the last time I was in a theatre, I was on stage rehearsing. When the last time I was supposed to be on stage, my sister died. But it's exactly like it has been for almost two years. I can't show that around Poppy.

Instead, I show another usher my ticket and they tell me which door to enter through. I impulsively bought a good ticket. Ten rows back from the front, aisle seat. From what I know about The Wiggles, this is the ideal spot. At various points of the show, members of the band walk through the audience. It also gives Poppy space to dance, which I know she'll do.

I absently plop down into my assigned red chair. The folded out bottom bounces under the force of me sitting. I laugh at myself and take in my surroundings. The classic plush theatre chairs, the ornate crown moulding around the balconies, the Roman-inspired mural spanning the entire ceiling. My stomach churns at the odd mix of feeling both out of place and at home.

Poppy tugs on the end of my ponytail and I almost reprimand her before I realize she's trying to get my attention. The man next to us has been staring.

"Oh," I say as I turn and meet those same eyes from yesterday.

"Hey," Theo says. "Again."

"Hey, again," I say. "Didn't expect to see you here."

"No, I imagine you wouldn't have," he says with a chuckle, then leans in closer to my ear and lowers his voice. "Emma's too cool for The Wiggles now, but my mom won tickets, so we had to go."

I smirk and glance at Emma, who, like Theo said, is trying very hard to look uninterested. Her long arms are folded across her chest and her lips are set in a pout. She's put as much space as possible between her and her father while still sitting next to him.

"I've heard they're very talented, if that helps," I say loud enough for Emma to hear. "Plus, she's probably much cooler than I am. This is my first concert since 2020."

"For real?" Theo asks, his bushy eyebrows shooting up. "You seemed like you were always going to concerts."

"I was," I say, surprised he remembered that. But I don't have time to dwell on the thought because Emma finally jumps into the conversation.

"My last concert was Pink," she says. She grins at me, right front tooth missing, somehow highlighting her left eye that is evenly split down the middle: half icy blue, half brown. This kid is definitely cooler than me.

"Okay, well, The Wiggles probably don't have the same acrobatics as Pink," I say with a shrug. "But a show is still a show. I used to go to every show I could."

Her eyes widen. "Really? Like what?"

I try to dig up artists from my memory that would impress a child in my mom's second-grade class. But seeing as I haven't gone to any popular shows in over three years, I'm shit out of luck.

"I've seen Taylor Swift a few times," I finally settle on.

When Iris and I were growing up, she always said I could be the next Taylor. I'd been writing songs for about as long as she had, playing piano and guitar since I was five and ten, respectively. Iris was always so confident I would see my name in lights. She was the one who suggested I apply to the RCM program after I sold my first song. She was convinced it would further my career, get me more training and visibility. She told everyone who would listen that I had sold my first song and was going to be a big star.

"That's amazing!" Emma yells. "I wish I was at her concert instead of this one. Have you ever seen Olivia Rodrigo?"

I smile politely. "I haven't seen her yet. Have you?"

"No, but a girl in my class saw her and said she was amazing. That's another concert I wish I was at instead."

I hold back a laugh at the obvious sass, and Theo shoots me an exasperated look, letting me know this is not an uncommon thing with his daughter. I immediately love her. She seems so much like a young me. Back when I was cool and sassy and yelled at the most popular boy in high school for dumping his coffee on the project I'd spent weeks slaving over. I meet Theo's eyes again. He probably doesn't even remember that.

"I do think this is a worthy first concert for Pops, though," I say, which prompts Poppy to wave at the mention of her name.

"Pops?" Theo asks.

"Poppy."

"Your mom's name is a flower too, right? And then Iris and Magnolia . . . Another flower?"

"Marigold. She usually goes by Goldie. But, yeah, keeping the tradition alive. My dad's a florist. Had a plan to open his own flower shop his whole life. He met my mom and they just clicked. It's this whole thing about how he found his favourite flower and they created a garden together, so that's why there's all the weird flower names in the family. Kind of a nauseating analogy . . ."

The easy smile spreads across his face again. "No, that's really cute." He turns his attention to Poppy and holds out his hand. She hesitates for a moment, then takes it and gives him her scrunch-nosed smile. "Hey, cutie. Who's your favourite Wiggle?"

Poppy holds out her plush, then hugs it to her chest again. "Doggy!"

"Wags is such a good choice!" Theo says. "You know, me and Emma have a real doggy named Rocket."

"Show them the picture, Dad," Emma says. "Rocket is the best. We rescued him from the Humane Society. He's three years old and has the same birthday as me."

Theo pulls out his phone and types in his password. I note that his background photo is a picture of him and Emma at a lookout point on a hike. The first photo in his camera roll is one of the dog. He turns the phone to me and scrolls through a few images. Rocket is a Bernese Mountain Dog with the classic white, black, and rust colouring. In every picture, his tongue hangs out. He almost looks like he's smiling.

"He's a prince," I say. "He looks like the sweetest boy."

"He is!" Emma confirms. "You should come meet him. He loves new people."

The lights dim and Theo leans into me again. "You definitely don't have to do that if you don't want to. But he is a very sweet boy. I'm sure he'd like you as well."

I flush and thank the dimming lights for masking the colour on my cheeks.

Chapter Four

September sneaks up on us and I just know that, like last year, it'll be my busy month with Poppy. My mom goes back to her second-grade class, and I go back to being the unpaid nanny of my sister's child. Summer is ideal. I have free rein to have my own life because Mom can hang out with Poppy more regularly. I'll still take her out because she enjoys the routine of being with me for most of the day, but when summer vacation ends, it's all me, all the time.

I feel like I've been hit by a ton of bricks. Maybe going to a concert on the last day of August made me forget about my impending return to full-time nanny duties. Maybe I wanted that distraction from the shambles that is my life.

It's not that I don't love Poppy, because I do. At this point in time, she is my world, no matter how pathetic that sounds. It's just that Poppy is such a stark reminder of Iris that she sometimes hurts to look at. She has Iris's olive skin, dark eyes, and daintiness, as if she were the dancer that Iris never was. She's got her personality on lock in that tiny body of hers and she adores nature, just like her mom did. There is never a moment where I don't wish Iris could be here to see her. But I get why Iris's boyfriend, James, walked away and gave custody to our parents. Through no fault of her own, Poppy's love hurts.

She climbed into my bed this morning when Mom left for school. I relish her cuddles against my neck. I relish the start of our days. But my heart hurts because this should be how Iris's days begin instead.

I reach beyond Poppy's head and pick up my phone. My goal is some mindless Instagram scrolling, but my notifications derail this plan. The first is a text from Mom, and I expect it.

Mom: Happy September 5th, honey! Hope you and Poppy have a great day. I still think you'd really enjoy teaching! The first day of school is always such a thrill. Hope you'll think about it this year. Xo

Every year, she sends me a text like this. Mom's biggest goal in life is to make me a teacher just like her. I recognize that my dreams were farfetched. Becoming a singer isn't something you do on a whim and expect to make it big right away. It takes planning and years of dedication. But I always had Iris to let me know my dedication was worth it, even if Mom didn't think so.

I send back a smiley face, then groan as I open my email.

"Lia sad?" Poppy asks.

I hadn't realized she was awake. I stroke the ringlets at the back of her neck. "Lia's excited to spend the day with you. What do you want to do?"

I'm late to work. My shift is five to midnight at the pub tonight, and I arrive at 5:15 p.m. Mom kept telling me all

the benefits that come with teaching, including the fact that it would be something productive I could do with my life, which is a thinly veiled judgement of me working at a pub. I'm not sure where else she wants me to work considering I have to watch Poppy until she or Dad gets home, and I have exactly zero relevant university education.

"Magnolia! Nice of you to join us!" Andy, my manager, muses as I saunter through the doors.

I throw him a peace sign as I pull my hair back into a ponytail. He rolls his eyes and gestures to the stage opposite the bar. It's karaoke night, and I'm in charge. The second he found out I had some sort of theatre background when I got the job last fall, he gave me all the special night duties. Trivia night and our speed dating event are also mine to host. I head to the back and pluck my apron off its hook, then tie it around my waist. The uniform here is wear anything, but you must also wear the UFO embroidered apron. That's how we do it at the UFO Pub. I'm honestly still a little disappointed they didn't lean fully into the alien theme, but at least the little green logo is cute.

I take a breath then walk back out. The dull throb of voices bouncing off the pub walls fills my ears. I've always loved the thrum of a crowd. The excitement and anticipation, even if it is just for karaoke. I step up on the elevated platform in front of the sequin wall and adjust the microphone back up to my height. At five-foot-ten, I'm always adjusting this microphone because every other person I work with is shorter than me, except for a few of the guys. The spotlights go up and focus on me. I zero in on the karaoke screen and shoot Zac, the only person on the UFO team who knows how to work the lights, a thumbs-up. The disco ball above me snaps on, sending rays of light in every colour of the rainbow all around the room.

"How are we feeling tonight?" I ask the bubbling room. Cheers and raised glasses show me what I already know. This rowdy little group is raring to sing some shitty karaoke. "That's what I like to hear! All right, y'all," I say and gesture at the table to my left. "This is the sign-up sheet. I see we already have quite a list forming. We'll have everything geared up and ready to go for you. All you have to do is stand up here and sing what's on there." I make a flourish toward the karaoke machine. "If you don't remember when your song is coming up, don't worry, I'll give a little announcement. Have fun tonight!" I bend to look at the list and laugh as I read off the first song. "First up, we have Aaron with 'Never Gonna Give You Up!' Give it up for Aaron!"

Polite applause erupts from most of the tables. I hand off the mic to a man who very much resembles your classic frat boy. I step off the stage and take a picture of the list on my phone, then grab one of three microphones we have and bury it in the front pocket of my apron. I use it to announce songs from anywhere in the pub, making my job much easier and much less stand-around-and-do-nothing. I have no idea how, but Zac has configured this specific wireless microphone to work anywhere in the pub and only pick up my words when I need it to. Though, I realize he probably has a very close handle on things and only turns it on when necessary. Whatever, I'll believe it's magic.

"Happy first day of school, Lia!" Chloe shouts as I settle in behind the bar.

I eye the French fries on the plate in front of her. "I'm not above throwing the fries at you, you know."

She smirks and picks up her order. "I do know," she says and sashays away to table three. "Which is why I won't let you."

I met Chloe in Europe last March. Ironically, while eating at a pub in Ireland. At the time, her hair was long and dark, save for the white chunk framing the right side of her face. I thought it was just a funky way she'd decided to dye her hair. Turns out it's a genetic disorder that affects pigmentation in hair, eyes, and skin. Now, her black-and-white hair is cut into a cute pixie. Her goal was to look like Alice Cullen, and you know what, she did it. We bonded over being from the same town. I finished the last month of my trip with her, then returned home to start my new life with Poppy.

Chloe didn't come back until August, but when she finally made her way home, she got me this job. And now a year later, Chloe is almost ready to head out on her next trip and I am still here.

I glance down at the karaoke list. "And now we have Megan and Josh with 'Start of Something New.' Bless you guys."

The first few bars from the *High School Musical* song begin to play. Chloe laughs as she walks back to me.

"There's always one, eh?" she says. "So, how was your first day of school?"

I sigh and busy myself by mixing up a margarita for an order that just came in. "It's just another day with Pops. We watched *Frozen* for the millionth time, and then made pancakes shaped like snowflakes."

"Damn, you're so talented!"

"Thank you. I take pride in my pancake art," I say with a laugh, then slide the marg away to its waitress.

"So what's bugging you, then?"

I sigh, then notice the song ending. I scroll to the list on my phone again. "That was beautiful, guys! For another throwback, we have Sara with 'You Belong With Me!'"

"Seriously," Chloe says, leaning against the bar, waiting for her order. "What's got you down today?"

"You say that like I'm always down."

She shrugs. "Well . . ."

I smirk and shake my head. "Have I ever told you about Maura? This girl I went to school with?"

"Was she your former secret lover?" Chloe wiggles her eyebrows, then she picks up the plates of nachos, spinach dip, and mozzarella sticks. "Hold that for a minute."

I watch her deliver the food to table seven, one that faces the parking lot. My stomach growls at the smell of all the greasy food. A pro and con about working here is that we can snag food from the back and eat it in our break room. I only do it once or twice a week, otherwise my stomach will hate me, bloat, and cramp. Tonight might be the night for all things fried. I eye a burger that's just appeared from the kitchen.

"Table four, babe," Jessie says.

I nod and head out to deliver the food. Once I reach the table, I announce the next song. Chloe meets me back at the bar.

"So, who's Maura?" she asks.

"Maura makes her Broadway debut next month. I just got invited to her opening night."

"Good for her! You're going, right?" When I don't answer, Chloe stops everything she's doing and stares at me. She just stares, trying to get me to crack because she has that power over people. "You're not going to go?"

"Well, with what money or time?"

"Your parents and Andy would not give two shits if you took a weekend off. And, dude, with the money you've made from here. I don't see you paying rent or blowing money on random shit."

"See, that is where you're wrong," I say, trying in vain to steer the conversation away somehow, even though I volunteered the info. "I buy a ton of random shit. I get suckered into those Instagram ads so easily, plus I get things for Poppy all the time, and—"

"You need to go back to singing, girl!" Chloe announces. Her eyes widen as she locks in on the karaoke stage. "In fact, I'm not taking no for an answer. Go. Sing."

Chloe drags me to the front of the pub, ignoring my excuses and pleas to stop. Tables of people look over as the previous song finishes. Suddenly, I'm on stage next to Chloe. The other girl . . . not Sara . . . maybe Winnie? She's gone. The music has momentarily stopped. Zac watches from the sidelines, hands hovering over buttons. Chloe adjusts the mic stand much lower to her height.

"There's been a slight change in order. Promise it won't take long," she charms the audience, playing with a string on the laced-up front of her top. "Our gorgeous and extremely talented host, Magnolia, is going to sing for you tonight! I sincerely hope you enjoy this because she is a damn good, trained professional."

Chloe readjusts the mic then steps down from the stage. She whispers something to Zac. He nods and types something into the computer attached to the sound system. Music begins to play from the speakers.

It's my song.

The crowd cheers, instantly recognizing it, and why

wouldn't they? It's a good song. It made favourites lists and even hit the *Billboard* charts the year it was released. But I haven't been on a stage and sung since Iris died.

I open my mouth to sing, then run off the stage.

Chapter Five

"Yes, I used up all the flour, but when is the last time you used flour?" I ask my mom through the phone.

Apparently, she needs flour for some project with her second graders. Seems like a lot of effort to go through during the first week of school, but hey, I'm not a teacher so what do I know? The call came in during Poppy's nap time, not quite demanding, but definitely more than simply asking me to go get some flour. Which turned into her asking me to pick up the groceries for the week.

"You're the baker in the family, honey," she says, which is true, but doesn't make me want to wake up a sleeping toddler and venture out into the rain. "You know I only make cookies at Thanksgiving and Christmas. Wouldn't you rather have some on hand for when you need it next?"

I sigh. Rain pelts the windows, just as it has since 8:00 a.m. "Can't you or Dad do it on the way home from work?"

"We could. But wouldn't it be better to have it now?"

I hate that she's right. Today is the kind of day where you stay in and make fresh, warm, homemade cookies. Today is not the kind of day where you run through the rain and become a drowned rat just to get ingredients.

"Okay, fine, I'll go get flour. But I'm not getting the rest of the groceries."

I'm fairly certain you have to be a psychopath to like grocery shopping. No offence to all the psychopaths out there who also dislike the chore. In all my twenty-five years, I have never enjoyed a trip to the grocery store. Add in a toddler, and you have a real winning combination.

Poppy is grumpy. Her idea of the perfect afternoon did not involve me putting her in a bright-yellow rain jacket that's about a size too big and pools around her little arms, taking her out into the freezing, entirely too windy rainstorm, and plopping her into a shopping cart that I didn't realize was also wet, subsequently starting a post-nap meltdown. To be fair, though, this is also not my idea of a perfect afternoon.

"Pops, all we need is flour and we can go, okay?" I say and smooth down the wet curls by her face. The hood of her jacket kept most of her hair dry, but with curls flying everywhere you're bound to get some of them wet.

Also, I lied. It's not just flour. It's all the groceries. Apparently, they were nonnegotiable.

"All right, Poppy, which way should we go?" I ask.

Poppy stares at me impassively. The amount of attitude in this tiny body of hers is ridiculous. They never tell you that about toddlers. They just let you stumble upon the hardcore sass all by yourself. She crosses her arms and adds in a pout and turned-up jaw for good measure. I sigh and look down at the list.

"Guess we'll get the produce first," I mutter to myself.

I turn left and scan the vibrant piles of fruits and vegetables. I park our cart in front of a stack of Red Delicious apples. They're not on the list, but I know I can appease Poppy and get her back on my side this way.

But Poppy also knows this. They're one of her favourite things to eat.

As I'm reaching for a bag, Poppy's quick raptor claws reach out and grab an apple from the bottom of the stack. Rule number one with a toddler is never turn your back. And I turned my back. The apples come crashing down, cascading from the top of the stack, falling over each other and careening to the floor where they roll away. I jump back as they keep falling and cover my mouth. Something between a laugh and a scream threatens to bubble out of me.

Poppy gleefully shows me her bright-red apple and takes a big bite out of it. She's either oblivious to or intentionally ignoring the apple storm around her.

"Oh my God," I whisper. My hand moves up to the bridge of my nose and I close my eyes. I can feel the heat from my cheeks. "Shit. Shit, shit, shit."

"Could be worse," a voice just behind me says. "She could have walked into a stack of spaghetti sauce, causing it to all fall down, break, and make the floor look like a murder scene."

I turn and eye Theo Hennessy. "Do you speak from experience?"

He bends down, picks up one of the apples, and shines it on his University of Toronto sweater. "Yes, I do. Emma scared the shit out of herself when she was just learning to walk. In hindsight, I probably should have held her hand or something, but she was having fun trotting along next to the cart, and I didn't think anything of it. Toddlers, man."

"No one tells you how wild they are. It's like you have a dog, but the dog is on drugs and the world is on fire, and they just want to show you how cool their poop is."

Theo stares at me open mouthed for a moment, then laughs. His laugh is the kind that takes over a room, just like it did in high school, often derailing classes when someone was joking around. I flush.

"Bad day?" he asks.

I reach forward and grab the Poppy-mobile. I steer it away from the apples, now settled on the speckled tile. A young man who looks barely twenty surveys the scene with something akin to horror.

"I'm so sorry," I say. He waves me off and I turn back to Theo. "Bad year."

"Really?" he asks. His eyebrows knit together, and he studies me as if he can tell. Given the fact that he knew me in my former glory, he probably can tell. It's not like anyone looks stunning after running through the rain. I've seen quite a few women in here with makeup running down their faces. But it's more the fact that I'm wearing a pair of leggings and a ratty old T-shirt with a clearly visible hole at the hem beneath my sodden jean jacket. I never would have been out in public like this a few years ago, and I definitely would have been wearing more colour. "Need an ear?"

I swallow, oddly touched. "I can't ask you to do that."

I lower my eyes and peek at Poppy, who is still munching away on her apple.

"I don't mind." He glances at my left hand and I curl my fingers around the handle of the cart. "I know what it's like to do this alone. I also know what it's like to have no one to really relate to about that . . ." He shrugs then smiles shyly. "Just an offer."

I return the smile and tuck a strand of damp hair behind my ear. "Well, thank you. That's really sweet of you to offer. However, I don't think I'm going to spill my guts in a grocery store."

"No, of course not," he says, the smile growing, becoming more certain, more genuine. "You have me on Facebook, I think, if you ever want to chat."

I nod. "I'm sure you don't want to talk about toddlers in your free time."

"Why not? Who wouldn't want to talk about dogs on drugs while the world's on fire, and what was it?"

"Poop."

Theo snaps his fingers, gaining Poppy's attention. "Ah, that's right. Poop." Poppy giggles. "Though, I'll pass on the poop. I talk about that enough at work."

I can't hold the laugh back this time. I shake my head and bask under the command of his chuckle that melts me like butter.

"I'm sorry, what do you do that you're talking about poop?"

"I'm a paramedic," he replies. "There's a surprising amount of poop talk in the back of an ambulance. Also, blood and other fluids, but yeah, poop."

"Noted. So just the dogs on drugs, then?"

"And the fire."

"I can bring all three of those things to the conversation table."

Chapter Six

"Hanna, I need you to tell me what to do," I say to the emptiness of my car and Hanna's disembodied voice on speaker phone. "Should I message him?"

"Okay, I have thoughts," Hanna replies.

"She has a lot of thoughts!" Drew yells from somewhere in the background.

I laugh as Hanna shushes him. Their easy dynamic is part of why I want to message Theo. Every time I've met him in the last few weeks, it's been easy. I've felt more like myself in those brief moments, kind of flirting with him, than I have in the last two years. And yet I can't help thinking about how much I know and don't know about him. I have a lot of perceptions about who he was, but I know how very wrong I could be, especially since he's been very personable in the present and those moments are really the only times I've had conversation with him that's deeper than saying hello.

"Okay, so first, tell me why we don't like him."

The truth is, I don't know. In high school, I took all the artsy courses because I knew I wasn't going to need math or science with my chosen career. Along with the obvious music class, I also took art. In grade eleven, one of our assignments was to create an album cover. We had to really think about it and come up with the title, track list, and a design that made sense with the overall vibe. We obviously didn't have to record it or anything, but it had to look real. It was our culminating project and I'd spent weeks on it. Theo was also in the class, and he was good but not great. I never really understood why he took the class considering all his other electives were science related and, to my knowledge, his goal in life was to become a doctor. But there he was, sitting in the row just behind me because our teacher sat us alphabetically.

On the last day of class, Theo dumped his coffee on my project. I was so mad he'd ruined it that I never knew if it was on purpose or a total accident.

"He wrecked my project," I say, pulling the Bug into my driveway and killing the engine. "But I don't think he meant to."

"Honestly, he doesn't seem like the type that would intentionally do that, Lia. I think we blew it out of proportion because we were stupid."

"Hey!"

"Stupid like young. What teenager isn't reactionary?"

"The lucky ones."

I tip my head back against the headrest. From this vantage point in the driveway, only one light is on in the house and it's in my parents' room. My mom typically goes to bed early on school nights, while my dad stays up. Because they're so disgustingly in love, even though one of them is asleep and one is awake, they usually stay in the same room together. Unless, that is, my dad is hanging out with me. But on nights I'm working, he's always with her. I'd be lying if I said I didn't want that.

"Okay, so this isn't important, but it is important . . . What does he look like now? He hasn't updated his Facebook since we graduated."

I sigh. "I don't know. He looks like himself, but with a beard." I pause and try to place his familiar face, then snap my fingers. "Oh! He looks like the guy who was on two-and-a-half seasons of *The Bachelorette!*"

"Blake?" Hanna says with a laugh. "He's from around here. Have you checked they're not related?"

"I forgot we're all related here in Canada."

Hanna waves off my comment and moves on to her next query. "Does he think you're Poppy's mom, though? Like, is he looking for a single mom to match his single parent-ness?"

I close my eyes and pinch the bridge of my nose. I'd thought of that too. I was actually quite certain he did think I was Poppy's mother. He's not the first person to assume that. She looks so much more like Iris, but she has my hair, and without Iris around, it's kind of hard to tell that she isn't my mini me. He is, however, the first person to assume that and then show interest in me.

"I think he might. I haven't really had a chance to tell him otherwise, and I understand when people make that assumption."

"Yeah, that's totally fair. But are you ready to be a step-mom if that's what he's looking for?"

"Is it possible he's just looking for someone? He's had a kid for seven years, most of those being when the rest of us were off having fun and dating people in university. I feel like he maybe missed that portion of his life."

Hanna considers this for a moment and makes a ponderous noise. "Another fair point. But are you in that point of *your* life?"

"I really don't know what fucking part of my life I'm in right now, Han."

Truer words have never been spoken. It is extremely tiring to not know where you're going. Life is paralyzing when you have no goal. And it's not like I'm about to tell people that my life goal, which I've worked toward for probably twenty years, has completely obliterated me and sent me spiralling to the great unknown destination of What-The-Fuck-Am-I-Doing-With-My-Life Land. What does it mean to fail when you've always been the one to know what you wanted?

Hanna laughs because she thinks I'm joking. I've never admitted it seriously that I'm lost. I've never told people that I stopped working on my dream the second my sister's heart stopped beating. Everyone thinks I'm working at the pub because that's what you do when you're in the arts and waiting for your big break. I'm the only one who knows I'm there because I don't know where else to go.

"Okay, so we don't know his intentions. That's fine, I guess, for now. Though, genuine question, is he stalking you? You keep running into him."

"None of the times I've run into him have been on purpose. Park was totally random, concert he had no way of knowing I'd be there, and grocery store he only noticed me when Poppy chose violence."

"All good things to know," Hanna says. A thread of excitement creeps into her voice. "Lia, please message him."

I laugh, taken aback by her sudden certainty in this man. "Why?"

"Well, aside from the fact that you like him enough to ask the question, this sounds like a romcom. You're having all these meet-cutes with him. Can't you just picture Julia Roberts or Meg Ryan meeting this bearded guy over and over again? This is the part of the movie where you jump at the chance and start messaging the hot guy. Then, eventually you guys have sex and kiss in the rain or snow and fireworks happen."

"That is quite the ending to a romcom. All at once? Are we having sex in the snow, under the fireworks?"

"Shut up," Hanna says with a giggle. "I just think a little romance might be good for you."

"I'm heading in. You should go to sleep."

"Promise me you'll message him!"

I pick my phone up from its spot in the cup holder and take Hanna off speakerphone. "I'll see what I can do."

I sit in silence in the car after the call. A curtain moves in my parents' room and the black-rimmed glasses that frame my dad's face briefly appear. I raise a hand on the off chance he can actually see into my car. The curtain whooshes back into place. My phone lights up with a text from Hanna, telling me to talk to Theo. I bite my lip and move to Facebook Messenger. I type his name and open a message thread I've never seen.

It's an apology for ruining my project. He sent it the night after that class. I pause on the message, then lock my phone. I open the car door.

I was wrong about Theo all those years ago.

Chapter Seven

Uncertainty kept me up last night. I debated sending the message countless times, but I didn't want him coming back to his messages and seeing the one I apparently ignored for eight years. Even if it wasn't intentional and I had no clue it even existed, sending another message made me think he would see the old one and assume I'd been petty. I mean, I can be petty, I just wasn't specifically in this instance. It just looked like it.

And so went my thoughts, spiralling until dull light slipped through the cracks in my blinds and told me a new day had arrived.

I sip on the travel mug of coffee as Poppy wanders around the kid's section of the library. She pulls out books with characters she recognizes from TV and movies, then hands them off to me to put in my library bag. It's the same ratty old red tote my mom used when she took me and Iris to the library when we were kids.

I peek at the time on my phone. I try to take Poppy to a day program at the library so she can interact with other toddlers every week, though sometimes it's every two weeks. I only know what time the programs start. I'm always surprised by what we end up doing. The spiciest thing in my life right now is guessing what Poppy and I will do on library program days.

The program leader, a woman named Anjali who is just slightly older than me with the most gorgeous glossy black hair, walks out from the program room. She scans the children's area of the library, brightly decorated with primary colours, train tables, and computers with games from my childhood. Parents with their toddlers mill around, chatting in hushed voices and watching their babies play together.

Poppy climbs onto a padded staircase as Anjali announces it's time for the program to begin. I follow Poppy's climb, placing my stainless steel mug down at the bottom of the staircase. She reaches the top triumphantly, arms stretched to the sky, and I grab her ankle. I give her a playful yank and she giggles.

"Come on, Pops, time to hang out with Anj," I say.

Poppy grins and scuttles down the stairs. I rush down to make sure she doesn't send my coffee flying. At the bottom of the stairs, she holds out her hand and waits for me to straighten and take it. I grasp her tiny hand in mine and squeeze three times, my family's coded version of *I love you*.

Inside the wooden walls of the program room are instruments. Tiny human-sized guitars, drums, tambourines, maracas, and microphones scatter the ground. I can't help the groan that escapes me as I realize today is a music day. As much as I adore music in every sense of the word and in every inch of my being, it's been a hard thing to love recently. But despite my hesitation, Poppy is overjoyed. Like every other child coming into the room, Poppy makes a beeline for the thing she thinks will make the most noise.

I sit down behind her, which is always the drill for these classes. Kids form the main part of the circle, adults in back. Poppy bangs her hands against the bongos, laughing every time the hollow sound rings out. I grin at her melodic giggle.

"Good job, Poppy!" I praise.

That's the part of music I love. The joy that kids find as they realize they can create something. That's generally the joy I used to find as well. Somehow, as I sit in this room of kids exploring and creating as I once had, the joy begins to seep back into my heart. And unintentionally, I tear up. I wipe at the corner of my eye and refocus on Poppy.

"Today, we are making music!" Anjali announces and holds up a shiny golden horn. "When I point to you, please make your mark on the world and let those instruments cry out!"

I hold Poppy's hands as each child has their chance to play their little heart out. She fights me at first, but eventually stops to listen to the others. She claps after each solo and I love her more and more for her grace. Finally, Anjali points to Poppy. She smashes her hands against the bongos, singing in her own made-up language. Once more, the tears come and I have to force myself to zone out.

A half hour passes as the kids learn about different instruments, make different sounds, and sing along to Anjali's nursery rhymes. I tune them out for the most part, determined to not cry and have all the moms ask me prying questions. I succeed and I also save a life. I mean, probably.

A little boy in a Super Mario T-shirt on the opposite

side of the class turns away from the circle. He clutches at his throat and scans the room with wide eyes, searching in vain for his person. I reach a hand forward and speak without thinking.

"Hey! Are you okay?" I yell across the circle, above all the noise.

The boy locks fearful eyes with me. He begins to cough and sputter. The two women on either side of him finally take their eyes off their joyful kids and notice what's happening. Their mouths open in wide *O*'s of shock while the boy begins to turn red.

"Someone help him!" one woman shouts.

"Call 911!" yells another.

Anjali rushes over to the boy and grasps his shoulder. She tries speaking to him, but he mimes he can't breathe. Can't speak.

"Where did his nanny go?" a third woman asks.

I hold Poppy, whose brow has furrowed in confusion. Her lower lip trembles and I draw her to my chest, sheltering her away from the stampede of moms trying to help this poor little boy. Other kids begin to cry and I sit, paralyzed with Poppy, unsure what else I can do.

"You found the EpiPen?" Anjali asks one woman over the dull throb of concerned voices. "Does anyone know how to use it?"

Someone bleats out instructions. I watch helplessly. I consider leaving with Poppy, taking her shaking body away from the chaos, but the doors are blocked by bodies. So I do the only thing I can: rub her back and assure her that everything is okay.

The commotion eases as the EpiPen begins to work,

but chaos starts up again as a small woman with sandy brown hair in a high ponytail slips in through the doors. She takes in the scene, the lack of music, the huddle of moms, her kid on the floor, and covers her mouth with her hands. She drops to her knees and covers her face. I hear words of both encouragement and shame. My head pounds to the sound of approaching sirens.

Moments later, the doors to the program room fly open. Two men and a gurney burst through. I recognize the bearded man with piercing blue eyes immediately. Of course.

Theo.

Chapter Eight

It's true what they say about a man in uniform. I try not to enjoy Theo's arms given the circumstances, but I fail. The uniform showcases the veins in his forearms and just the bottom of his bicep peeking out below the medical insignia embroidered on the shoulder of his shirt as it strains while he prepares the stretcher.

Theo bends down and speaks to the child. The child seems to have levelled into a functioning human again since the EpiPen was found, even as far as smiling. I'm not entirely familiar with allergic reactions or assessments from medical professionals, but I assume Theo is mentally checking off a list as he talks with the little boy. I can't help but admire Theo's admittedly firm-looking backside from my vantage point. The lifting and squatting from his job have obviously done him good.

Theo's partner, a tall man with tight curls and frosted tips, talks with the surrounding mothers. One points to me and I blink rapidly, trying to figure out how I fit into this before my annoyingly Theo-scattered brain realizes I was the one to spot something wrong with the boy. The partner nods along to the conversation, then calmly turns to the nanny. He reaches out and places his hands on her shoulders, steadying her, then gestures down to the boy sitting on the floor, but her sobs continue.

"I should have been here!" she cries. Her voice rings out in the wooden walled room as everyone settles down. Most of the moms watch from afar, their hands firmly guarding their children. "I don't even know where he would have found a peanut, much less eaten it! But he wouldn't have done it if I was in the room!"

I don't catch the reply, but her shoulders slump and she nods. The paramedic releases her shoulders and smiles at her reassuringly. She takes a deep breath, then crouches down to the child's level. The boy gives her a thumbs-up, and from what I can tell, she forces a smile, but not before she cringes at the red bumps that cover his arm. My heart goes out to her. If something ever happened to Poppy when I was supposed to be near her, I would die. Which sounds dramatic, and obviously I wouldn't literally die, but I've felt so completely certain that Poppy is my responsibility since Iris's death that any little thing would hurt me. And also probably make Iris roll in her grave.

I stand at the same time as Theo with Poppy still clinging to my chest. It's unintentional, but the movement on the opposite side of the room, the side that most of the moms have vacated in favour of chaos, draws his eyes to me. He pauses with his hand on the stretcher, recognition colouring his gaze. He looks down, briefly, cheeks reddening, then reverts his attention to the job at hand.

Did I make him blush? Was it because he caught me watching or is this, just like Hanna had said, another meet-cute? I chew on my lip as I figure out what to do. The question of whether I should leave is even more present in my mind, and it seems like I'm not the only person in the room questioning their next move. Though, I hope I'm the only woman in the room questioning if I should go up to Theo.

"Let's go for a ride, bud!" Theo announces to the young boy and the room. "Rolling beds are how kings travel all the time. If I could just lie down, relax, and be wheeled around, I totally would."

Poppy pulls herself away from my neck, hands on her cheeks, ready to cover her eyes should she need to. But just as I had noticed right away when Theo walked in, Poppy seems to recognize his voice and zeroes in on him. Her face lights up. She points to Theo as he high fives the little boy, who is now on the stretcher.

"Friend!" Poppy yells. "Apple Friend."

A giggle escapes me, and I cover my mouth at a few raised eyebrows. The judgemental looks flicker away after a moment, and I nuzzle Poppy.

"Yes, Pops!" I whisper. "Smart girl! That is our apple friend."

And even though I don't know Theo all that personally, suddenly the only thing I want to do is tell him that he's our apple friend. This time, it's my turn to flush. Oh fuck. I like him.

Theo and his partner head toward the door, the nanny trailing behind the king's rolling bed. Anjali leads the room in a round of applause, which gets the kids back into the playful sound-and-music-making mood. There are twenty minutes left of the ninety-minute program period. I pick at a nail, unintentionally drowning out all other conversation. Then, I catch Theo's eyes as he rounds the corner and out of the room. I sigh.

All right, here we go.

I thank Anjali for today but let her know we're ducking out early. She understands, and a few others leave with me as well. That small crowd ambles out of the room, while I walk as fast as possible without drawing too much attention to myself. I rush through cherry wood shelves of books, keeping Theo, his partner, and the stretcher in my eyeline. It doesn't take long to reach the large and slightly imposing wooden doors of the library. I jog up to them, jumping at my chance to finally help out. I push one door open as the nanny grunts and throws her weight against the opposite one. Poppy, albeit not helpful at all and throwing me off balance just a bit, reaches out to help me hold my door.

"Thank you!" says Mo, Theo's partner, as I finally spot his name badge.

They push through the doors and Theo reaches out to me, clapping me on my shoulder as he passes. He also gives me the most delicious wink. I steel myself against the door because my knees go a little weak. When the doors close behind me and the nanny, I walk with her.

"You okay?" I ask her. She doesn't answer me at first, so I offer more. "I'm Magnolia, by the way. Don't think I've said that formally. And this is Poppy."

Poppy waves and gives her a scrunch-nosed smile because her only job in life right now is knowing when she's called upon to be cute.

The nanny smiles in spite of herself and wipes away a stray tear. "I'm Zoey and that's Luca."

"He's a trooper," I say.

"He shouldn't have to be."

"Hey, you did nothing wrong," I tell her as we come up next to the ambulance. Theo and Mo load Luca into the back, joking along with him as they do. "We all have moments where we step away for one second and something happens."

"I could have killed him," Zoey whispers.

The horror on her face extends much deeper than someone worried about her job. She loves this little boy like her own, which is exactly how I feel about Poppy.

I shake my head. "You knew what to do. You were prepared for something like this to happen and left him in a room with competent adults. You told someone you were leaving, right?" She nods. "Then you did nothing wrong. For all we know, someone could have eaten peanut butter just before this, then used one of the instruments. I'm so sorry this happened, but it's not your fault and, thank God, it ended really, really well. He's having a blast pretending he's king of the world!"

"Thank you," she says with a noise that may or may not be a laugh.

Theo walks up to us with the slightest bounce in his step. "Okay, Zoey, so you can come with us or you can drive behind us. Whatever you think Luca would be most comfortable with."

"I'll ride with you if you don't mind."

Theo steps aside for Zoey to pass. She smiles at me, then runs at full tilt to the back of the ambulance. I would have laughed at the enthusiasm in a different situation.

"That was quite a pep talk," Theo says. I turn my attention back to him just as he finishes writing something on a little pad. I don't have time to ask or wonder what he's doing. He rips the paper off the pad and hands it to me. "I gotta head out, but we keep bumping into each other and . . . yeah . . ." He rubs a hand on the back of his neck and makes an awkward, breathy sort of laugh. "Well, call or text me, okay?"

I glance down and find his phone number. "Oh. Okay."

Theo jogs to the ambulance, slams the back doors shut, then finds his place in the driver's seat. He waves as he flicks on the lights and siren. Poppy waves her arms enthusiastically, like most children do when they see an emergency vehicle.

"Apple Friend!" she yells.

Apple Friend.

Chapter Nine

"Okay, so he's in the middle of a whole emergency and he took the time out of his day to give you his number?" Hanna gushes at the pub later that night. "Girl, marry him."

"I'm not going to marry him for giving me his number," I say with a laugh and plop a thick golden fry into my mouth.

It's my break at work and I'm eating a makeshift dinner of French fries and garlic bread. I'd texted Hanna an SOS on my drive here and she immediately sent a string of question marks back, then after her shift ended at the hospital, she headed over. Now, sitting on a stool at the bar, I see the same elation on her face as when she and Drew first started dating.

"You know I don't mean that literally," she says with an eye roll. "But, come on. He likes you, Lia. He's making an effort to keep in contact with you. And honestly, the universe is, like, trying to destiny the two of you so hard, so I need you to act on this."

I sigh. "I dunno. On the one hand, yes, because he's cute, he's good with kids, he seems really sweet, and you're right, he is making an effort to keep in touch. But on the other hand, I feel like an idiot for holding a grudge against him for so long and I just . . . Am I capable of falling for someone again?"

Hanna takes a sip of her craft beer and ponders my question. She narrows her eyes at the brick wall of the bar, then turns to me.

"Give me a refresher. What would make you incapable of love?"

I shrug noncommittally and disguise my answer by taking a long swig of water. Can't drink on the job. "I don't know."

But I do. I know I'm scared to put my heart on the line for someone who might die on me. I have no control over who the universe deems apparently unimportant in growing old with me.

"Is this—Is this about everything two years ago?" Hanna asks, gently.

I try not to react at the veiled mention of Iris. So few people ever bring her up anymore that I inhale sharply, almost as if Hanna had cursed. And maybe that's why no one ever talks about her. Because even a vague reference to her hurts me and I'm half a second away from crying on this bar stool. I clear my throat and nod.

"Yeah, it might be," I admit, barely above a whisper.

Hanna lays her hand over my forearm. I study her freshly painted olive nails that complement her skin, polish she can only keep until one chip happens due to sanitary reasons. Her thumb rubs against my wrist.

"I miss her too," Hanna says. Her tone matches mine.

"She was the ultimate hype woman."

"She really was."

"But that doesn't mean she'll be the only person to ever hype you up in your life." She removes her hand from my arm, which somehow forces me to look at her face. "Look, I get how you're feeling. I get why you went to Europe and stopped singing. I get why so much of yourself slipped away after everything. Because she wasn't supposed to die. She was supposed to come home with Poppy, marry James, and live her life, but that didn't happen. It doesn't mean you have to stop living your life, though."

"I know."

I let the silence sit between us because I don't have anything more to say that won't completely break me. I can't explain how my world stopped revolving the second Iris's heart stopped beating. It just did. Everything changed, and I still haven't figured out how to navigate a world where she's dead and I have to go on as if everything is okay.

"You deserve to have other people hype you up, Lia."

"I know."

"Then text him. Because now I'm invested, and I think you need to make this jump."

Hanna nudges my phone toward me. When I don't move to pick it up, she continues to push it until it's almost falling off the edge of the chipping oak bar top. I pick it up but slide it inside my apron pocket. Hanna frowns at me then waves Chloe over.

"Chloe, tell Lia she needs to text the boy."

Chloe sets her sights on me. She leans against the bar

then crosses her arms over her chest, popping out just a smidge extra cleavage in her push-up bra and deep V-neck.

"I didn't know there was a boy. Lia's been holding out on me!"

I blush. "There is no boy. Yet."

"You have been flirting with him for, like, two weeks. There is a boy."

Chloe's mouth drops open in mock shock. Her hand dramatically comes to her chest. "Two weeks and I know nothing? You *have* been holding out."

"I haven't said anything because it wasn't anything until a few days ago."

"See!" Hanna says, triumphantly. "There is a boy and it is a thing!"

Hanna slips her hand into my apron pocket so swiftly, I don't even notice until my phone is in her hands. Chloe delights in this action and gratefully takes the phone from Hanna when I dive for it.

"Jokes on you guys. I'm password protected."

"1211," Hanna says simply.

Chloe enters the password into my phone, and it unlocks. She raises her eyebrows at Hanna, and I lower my gaze to the bar.

"Okay, you got me. It's Poppy's birthday. But what's your next move? His number isn't in there."

Chloe narrows her eyes and shifts to my contacts. She scrolls through, searching for any male name she doesn't recognize, pausing on a few to ask, then slumping her shoulders further as Hanna or I explain who they are.

"Well, fuck," she says. "Lia's right. Nothing we can do."

"Where did you put his number?" Hanna screeches.

"I would love to know the answer to that, but I have to get back to work, so just give me the CliffsNotes on who this guy is."

Hanna does exactly that. She goes into the four apparent meet-cutes I've had with Theo, then explains that we knew each other in high school, but weren't friends. Chloe nods along, but her interest wanes once Hanna reveals Theo is a single dad to a seven-year-old. Which makes sense considering Chloe isn't big on children and the DILF vibes do nothing for her.

"She should text him, right?" Hanna concludes.

Chloe hesitates, staring down at the bar where she's absently drawing shapes with her index finger. My heart pounds as I await her answer, which is precisely when I realize I'm going to text him regardless of what she says because I've somehow already gotten myself attached enough that rejection would hurt. Eventually, Chloe's internal war ceases and she meets my face with a halfhearted smile.

"You need to make the jump, I agree. You should text him. Just make sure he's not looking for a mom immediately."

And with that, she glides away. At Chloe's retreating back, I reveal my final secret of the night and pull Theo's little slip of paper out the front pocket of my jeans. I'd stuffed it in there the second he gave it to me, too worried that Poppy's grabby fingers would rip it up. Then, too worried I'd lose it if I left it in my room. There was an easy solution to the fear and that was putting his number into my phone, but that felt too permanent. I straighten the piece of paper on the bar top.

"Here's his number," I say, and Hanna breaks into a grin. "What do I say to him?"

"Just say, 'Hey, it's Magnolia!' You know, something easy like that. It doesn't have to be groundbreaking. Plus, if you start like that, you can see if he's a dry texter or if he comes up with anything creative."

I sigh then slide off the bar stool. My break ended about ten minutes ago but no one noticed or said anything, presumably because they were too busy to find me, and I ducked every time I saw someone other than Chloe. I grab my phone from Hanna's outstretched hand and finally enter his number into my contacts.

I type and retype a message, glad he doesn't have my number yet so he can't see the dots appearing and disappearing at the bottom of the screen. Hanna peers over my shoulder to see what I'm doing, but she doesn't interject. Finally, I settle on exactly what Hanna suggested. My fingers hover over the send button. I don't press it until Hanna gives me a gentle nudge.

"Okay," I breathe. "All sent."

"I await the impending SOS when he responds."

Chapter Ten

Theo texts me before I leave work. Hanna reads the message as I internally, and maybe, possibly, externally freak out. It's nothing major, but it's a message and it's enthusiastic and he is the first person to be interested in me in two years and I kind of want to throw up. I also kind of want to dance around and let everyone know the guy I like likes me back, but that's kind of weird, isn't it?

Hanna tells me to be chill and not message back until the morning. I get this advice, especially since the next time I'd get a chance to text him back would be after midnight once I'm driving home from work, so I nod along and agree.

But then I send another text back in the driveway of my house.

It's nearly 2:00 a.m., and I realize it's not an acceptable hour after I send it. Not that it ever was an acceptable hour since I got off work late anyway. But now he knows the hours I keep, and they're probably not the same as him considering his message came in at 9:42 p.m. A simple and cute little message.

Theo: Hey! Glad you messaged. Sorry to spring my number on you and then leave.

> **Magnolia:** Don't worry about it! I honestly hesitated to interrupt what you were doing as well. Guess I'm glad I did.

I cringe, reading my message once again as I sit in my car. What's the trick where you get your message back? Put it on airplane mode? But that only works the second after you send it, and it has been way longer than a second. Even though no one can see me and, really, it's not quite as forward of a message as I think, I still blush furiously. The heat in my face is so bad that I have to step out of my car and into the cool night air.

As I slam the door to the Bug, my phone buzzes. Immediately, I feel like a teenager again because my heart literally skips a beat.

Theo: I think I already said it . . . But just in case I wasn't clear enough, I'm glad you followed me out too ;)

I stand in the driveway, grinning like an idiot at my phone. My stomach does a flip flop and my whole body feels like it's tingling. My first instinct is to rush inside and show Iris the texts, my general response to anything boy-related from ages fourteen to twenty-three, but reality comes crashing in and my heart sinks into my butterfly-filled stomach. I can never tell Iris anything ever again.

I exhale and glance down at my phone screen. His message remains there, along with those infamous three dots. I wait with bated breath for his next message.

Theo: It's late. I'll message you in the morning. Go to sleep.

❊♪❊

We text almost constantly over the weekend. I sneak peeks at my phone so often while I host a special Saturday Trivia Night that a table calls me on it. And then Andy makes Chloe hang onto my phone for the rest of the night. But none of them outright complain. They never knew me before Iris died, but there's something about me that's been different. Happier.

Maybe. I haven't quite figured it out yet. Hanna thinks it's because I'm finally letting myself experience *it* again, though I'm not entirely sure what I'm experiencing considering we've been texting for about two days.

"What're you smiling at?" Dad asks over breakfast on Sunday.

I've always been easy to read. Acting was never going to be my thing, which is why I chose singing, I guess. I'm good at emoting, which is the best possible thing you can do as a singer. It makes your audience relate more to what you're doing. But I'm terrible at hiding how I'm truly feeling. Hence, all the sad girl vibes over the last two years. Even if I won't talk about it, everyone knows how I'm feeling.

And I've been terrible at hiding the Theo feels. That thought about playing it cool when you start a new relationship . . . Yeah, that's not me.

Mom turns around from her place at the sink, a dish towel hanging from her hands. She raises her eyebrows then grins. "You're blushing!" she exclaims and pulls out the chair next to me and Dad. "Who is he, Magnolia?"

I laugh, awkwardly, which makes Poppy giggle. "I don't know what you're talking about."

"I think you do!" Mom says. She reaches out and brushes the top of my nose with her finger. I pull back a second too late. "I know my little flower girl. That is a boy smile. Who are you texting? Where did you meet him? Tell me everything, Lia."

Much as I try to pretend it's not true, my mom is one of my best friends. Usually, I tell her everything and she gets excited about it right along with me. But for some reason, I just want to keep this between me and Poppy for a little bit longer.

"Magnolia," Dad says, eyeing me over the top of his black-rimmed glasses. He places the paper down on the table, allowing me a full view of his rose-printed tie. He has about one hundred different ties with flowers on them that he wears every day. The rose is a common one, overrated, in his opinion. "Is there a boy?"

I open my mouth to answer and probably tell a bit of a lie, but Poppy gets there first.

"Apple Friend!" Poppy squeaks, pointing to the slices on her plate.

My parents turn their heads toward her in unison, both with raised eyebrows and questions on their faces.

"Apple friend?" my mom is the first to ask. "What does that mean?"

We all wait for Poppy to explain, well aware that her two- to three-word sentences have no way of encompassing what an apple friend is, only that she has one. In spite of myself, I smile, glad that she likes him. But I know the rapid-fire questions are coming my way in only seconds.

"Magnolia, what does she mean?" Mom asks.

My phone buzzes against the table again and I flip it facedown before Mom can see Theo's name on the screen. I pop a piece of toast into my mouth to give myself time to think, and Mom rolls her eyes at my obvious diversion.

"Did I not tell you?" I say with a mouth full of crumbs. "Poppy knocked down an entire display of apples at the grocery store."

Poppy beams in pride, as if remembering and admiring her artwork of mass destruction.

"And you met someone while the apples were falling?"

"No," Poppy decides to speak up. "Doggy concert. And Poppy park."

Mom draws her eyes slowly over to me. She cocks her head then props it up with her hands on her chin, giving me her best tell-me-more face.

"I will give you one thing to go on," I say, push my chair away from the table, and pocket my phone as I stand. "Yes. All of those things."

"Magnolia! That is nothing!" my mother hisses jokingly.

"Yes."

I stand just behind my chair. We each have a specific spot around the kitchen table with one chair always left intentionally empty. I dig my fingernails into the black faux leather. Dad watches me in amusement while Mom just waits with that classic motherly disapproval face. Twenty-five years and it still makes me crumble.

"So, yeah, maybe there's a guy. But it's nothing right now. That's all you get. No more details until I actually go out with him."

"Do we get to meet him?" Dad asks. That's always his question with my potential boyfriends and it always makes me squirm. Not because I have a habit of dating bad guys, but because my family has a habit of embarrassing good guys. And me.

"No, not now."

I take my plate to the sink and listen to my parents mumble behind me. I already know they're coming up with a plan on how to trap me into saying more and bringing him over here.

"Besides, I'm on my way out now. Hanna needs some help decorating today, so we're going on a HomeSense date."

"I bet Hanna knows more than us," Mom says, baiting me.

I walk to the front door, then peek my head around a column in the front foyer that obscures the view into the kitchen. My parents are still looking at me. I slip my feet into a pair of leopard-print booties. It may still feel like summer outside, but it's September so I'm calling it fall.

"Yeah, I bet she does," I say with a smirk as I wave, then slip out the front door.

On the porch that wraps around the front of our house, I finally pull out my phone. Two texts from Theo await me. The one I read when Dad asked who was making me smile, and a new one.

Theo: I actually have zero plans today and I'm very thankful. Weekends can get super busy with all of Emma's hobbies

Theo: Which reminds me . . . Would you like to come to the stables with us on Saturday? Emma has a lesson where she's allowed to bring a friend and she'd like to show you guys Rocket.

I stare at the text. I want to ask him if this is a date, but I don't want to be too presumptuous, especially since it involves his kid. I don't work next Saturday and Poppy loves every animal on earth, even insects. Though they're five years apart, it seems like Emma and Poppy could get along really well, and it seems like Emma at least agrees enough to invite us out. Unless that's Theo's doing, which might be even more flattering, now that I think of it.

I don't let myself overthink it.

        Magnolia: I'd love to join. Text me the details!

Chapter Eleven

As I drive to the horse ranch, aptly named The Ranch, I question my outfit for the hundredth time. I've never ridden a horse and I don't intend to today, but I still wanted to dress the part. That's not to say I went full-on cowgirl, but that's also not to say I avoided that vibe. I picked out my favourite pair of high-waisted dark-wash jeans, mostly because they make my ass look good, and then switched shirts for about an hour. My mom laughed from the hallway once she realized what I was doing. And now, having finally decided on a basic tank top since it's still warm enough, and my fashionable brown riding boots (that have never seen a farm), I question the jeans.

It rained last night. What if I get them all gross and muddy?

I pull into a stony drive, old wooden fences lining each side. A large barn with grey wood and a forest-green roof sits at the end of the drive, which opens up into the parking lot. Next to the barn is the long wooden stable, decked out in similar colours as the barn. The lot isn't terribly busy. Unsurprisingly filled with a mix of pickup trucks and fancy cars, the appropriate horse demographic. Naturally,

I sandwich the Bug between a pickup and a BMW.

I don't hesitate to exit the car. I jump out, smelling the crisp, pre-rain, earthy notes of the air, thankful for a humidity break. I slip the scrunchie off my wrist and pull my long hair back into a ponytail.

Poppy kicks her feet when I open the door. I've hyped up this outing all week, annoying my mom to no end as Poppy continued to get more and more excited.

"Are we going to see some horsies, Pops?" I ask her.

In response, she lets out an ear-piercing screech. I'm pretty sure I go deaf for a moment, considering my ear was right next to her little mouth as I undid her car seat's belts. I pull out of the car and shake my head, then hear a chuckle.

Theo stands about ten feet away from me, hands in the pockets of his equally dark jeans, sleeves of his plaid shirt bunched up at his elbows. His lips quirk in a small smile and his eyes are bright, playful.

I return the smile and quip, "Enjoying the view?"

I bend more consciously into the Bug, intentionally angling my back in a way that makes my butt pop more as I free Poppy from her prison. With one arm I grab her, with the other I pull out her diaper bag. It's moments like these where my hands are completely full that I realize just how much I admire the work that parents, and probably more specifically, single parents do.

"Not gonna lie, I did," Theo says as I nudge the door closed with my hip. I sidle up to him and we walk at the same pace toward the back of the stables. "But I also remember the days when a child screamed in my face. Do you need any help?"

I shake my head. "No, I'm good. Got a good balance system this way."

He laughs, then fidgets with his hands as if he's not quite sure what to do. Would he hold mine if I wasn't acting as a pack mule? I bite my lip. Is he as nervous as I am? Is there any reason to be when we've so seamlessly been texting, and even talked on the phone once, for a whole week?

"Where's Rocket?" I ask, breaking the silence.

Theo exhales and I physically feel him relax beside me. My heart beats faster as he somehow endears himself even more to me.

"He's over with Emma. Thought I'd check to see if you guys got here. Glad I did. But Rocket is very excitable. I left him with her so he wouldn't run at you as you exited the car. Which he has done before to my grandma, and she wasn't pleased."

I laugh. "I can assure you, I wouldn't mind."

Poppy whispers, "Doggy" into my neck. Even though she apparently loves her apple friend enough to talk about him all the time at home—and girl, same—she's playing shy right now. I nuzzle her out into the world and she grins at Theo, then fits herself back underneath my chin.

"We're right over here," Theo says.

He points to a group of eleven girls all around the same age, standing next to a woman in leggings and very professional-looking boots, who I can only assume is their instructor. Parents mill around in the back, chatting politely with each other or staring at their phones. Half the girls hold their velvet horseback riding helmets under their arms while a few glance around uncertainly, hopping from foot to foot, clearly letting me know who takes the lesson and who's the guest. For the first time I wonder why

Emma invited us instead of someone her own age, but I don't consider it for long because a dog is running at me. I steel myself as eighty pounds of fluff and slobber tear toward me at full speed.

Rocket is definitely an appropriate name.

He jumps at my legs, and I drop the diaper bag. I have to dig my heels into the muddy ground to keep my hold on Poppy and not completely topple over. I reach a hand down to Rocket, burying my fingers into a mass of black and rust fur. He leans into me at the same moment Poppy leans away from me to get to the dog, and I finally lose the balance I've been struggling to keep.

A curse stops short on my lips and all that comes out is a soft, "Oh."

My back collides with something solid and warm, and hands clamp down on either side of my upper arms to steady me. I blush furiously at Theo's electric touch. My flesh rises in goosebumps and tingles where his hands lie. I breathe him in for a wholly unacceptable amount of time, basking in a mixture of scents: something between chocolate, grass, and a subtle hint of rain. The only thing that breaks me away from the shock of him is Rocket licking Poppy's leg, causing her to kick me.

I jump away with an "oof." Out the corner of my eye, I see Emma smile and realize I'm in one of those Hallmark movies that would play my song in the background where the child tries to hook up her dad. And I'm even more surprised to find out I don't mind. I turn to Theo, who looks at me almost shocked and playfully flexes his fingers.

"Thank you," I say. Poppy signs the phrase because The Wiggles taught her how, but also because she's not quite at the talking-to-strangers stage and probably doesn't understand why I'm thanking him.

Theo reaches down and collects his dog's leash. "Rocket, ladies and gentlemen." The group of girls, except for Emma, turns away. Theo leans closer to me and whispers, "Grandma wasn't fond of that. I wasn't close enough to catch her."

"Ouch," I whisper back as the instructor begins to speak to the girls. "Seriously, thank you. I would have landed right in the mud and probably ruined the whole day. Because I would absolutely complain about the mud and broken tailbone"

Theo chuckles. "I should have let you fall then," he says, and my mouth drops open. "Could have played doctor."

My mouth does not close. I look down at my mud-tipped boots and stifle a laugh. Theo's eyes bore into my skull hard enough that I'm forced to look up and meet the intensity in them. I raise my eyebrows. I turn back to the group and hear Theo exhale deeply behind me. I peek over my shoulder and smirk, and God, I am so glad he's not nervous anymore. Nervous Theo may have been endearing, but this. I like this side of him too.

It takes all my energy to focus on the riding instructor. Theo stands just behind me. I can almost feel his breath and I can certainly smell what I've learned is his scent. Now that I know what his skin feels like against my skin, I want nothing more than to back up and be in his embrace. But I am a cultured young woman, and I don't give in that easily. Much as I may want to engage in some PDA, I won't. Especially since his daughter and my niece are watching.

Poppy tugs at the neckline of my shirt, forcing me to look down at her then over at the majestic and gigantic animal that the instructor must have brought out when my head was in the clouds. I can't say I know horses well, but I think this is a Clydesdale. He's taller than me and Theo, intimidating, but none of the girls, including Poppy, seem to feel this way. They all gather around the horse, and I walk closer only because Poppy is straining so hard in my arms. I don't dare put her down next to the horse's white-tipped feet.

"This is Ross," the instructor explains. "We won't be riding with him today, but he loves attention so I thought I'd bring him out for a visit anyway." She holds out a carrot and the horse takes a big bite.

I step back, shocked at the crunch, and once more find myself against Theo's chest. This time I don't move away.

"All right, girls, we're going on a trail ride around the property. Parents can come if they want, but definitely do not have to."

With that, she turns and walks toward the stable. The girls follow. Emma turns to her dad, and they have some sort of unspoken conversation. He raises his eyebrows and tilts his head toward the stables. She shakes her head and holds her hand up flat. He nods. Emma runs to catch up to the rest of the girls.

"I see you have telepathy," I say and bend down to pat Rocket in a more relaxed manner. He's sitting pertly next to Theo's leg, pretending he didn't just try to ruin my favourite jeans.

"To some degree, I guess," he says with a shrug. "I'm sure you have that with Poppy, though."

Poppy delights in the mention of her name. She slinks out of the crease of my neck and buries her hands in Rocket's fur. For being not quite two years old, Poppy is surprisingly gentle with animals. Rocket turns and licks her arm, forcing a giggle to bubble out. Poppy detaches herself from me and plants her butt right next to Rocket, and I know she's done for the day. This is her new best friend, and she won't be moving until it's time to go or Rocket decides to love on another human.

"Look at that, Rocket! You made a new best friend!" Theo exclaims and his dog barks joyfully before licking Poppy's face.

I sigh and feel the ground beneath me. Thankfully, not as wet or muddy as the puddle I nearly fell into, and far more filled in with grass. I sit between Rocket and Poppy. Both seem to approve of this development, as Rocket lies down and leans into me and Poppy grins while continuing to pet him. Theo takes my lead and sits next to me.

"So, Theo Hennessy," I say, and his full name gets his full attention. "Been a while, hasn't it?"

He gives me an odd, questioning sort of look. "I guess it has been."

I laugh, awkwardly. "Yeah, I know that's a weird topic. But isn't it always a little weird when you run into someone from high school?"

"And here I was hoping we were doing more than just running into each other."

I look down as a blush creeps up my neck, but not before noticing the tips of his ears going red too. "I think you know we have been. But I guess I'm also kind of wondering why."

"Why?"

"Yeah, I mean, it's not like we really talked to each other back then. I honestly didn't even know you knew my name."

"You think I'd forget you after you called me a

handsome idiot?"

"I did not say that! When did I say that?!"

"Okay, you didn't say that directly, but you did ask me if I thought I was so attractive it gave me an excuse to be an idiot, which is basically the same thing."

My cheeks flame. I don't remember what I said to him when he wrecked my project, but clearly he does. And I don't doubt that I said it. It sounds like something I would yell in frustration, especially to someone like him in high school. But I'm learning... Maybe he wasn't who I thought he was then.

"Well, I'm sorry for—"

"No, don't apologize for that. It's all history. But also, you don't get to apologize for calling me hot."

I laugh, unabashed. "I wasn't going to apologize for that. I just— I think I thought you were someone else in high school. You had this... reputation."

"Oh, you mean the one about the hockey team being horny bastards?" Another laugh escapes me, one I try to hold back. It shocks me when it comes out in full, with an added snort. But I nod. He runs a hand over his face and shakes his head. "That is true for any teenage boy. But the specific rumour about having sex with, well, probably everyone, is not true. It's true for maybe two of the guys, though they could have been lying. They couldn't stop bragging in the locker room about all the girls they'd been with, and maybe people heard them doing that. I'm not sure. I never said anything about it because it somehow seemed to make me more desirable? Which I know is incredibly shallow, but what teenage boy doesn't want groupies?"

"Groupies? Really?" I say and fix him with a withering

stare. He shrinks back slightly and bites his lip.

"Yeah, not groupies. But you definitely were not one of them, and I liked that about you. I liked when you took me down a notch and made me realize I couldn't lean into that. I couldn't spill hot chocolate on someone's project and expect them to be okay with it by flirting my way out."

"I always thought it was coffee."

Theo wrinkles his nose. "I would never. Coffee is disgusting."

"That's sacrilegious!" He holds his hands up in surrender, making me laugh. "If it makes you feel any better, you still have groupies."

I flip my ponytail to my other shoulder, slyly looking at two of the moms behind me. They'd been eyeing Theo from the moment I walked in today.

"Single moms like single dads," he whispered, not even bothering to look at them. He leans closer to me and if Poppy weren't between us, I'd kiss him. "But I like a little more connection than that."

"Do you?" I whisper back.

"Yeah, I like women with a little bit of a spark," he says and reaches a hand out to my arm, tracing circles along my wrist. My skin certainly feels that spark with him. "Not that they don't. I'm sure they're lovely people. But they've never talked to me about anything other than their daughters or Emma. I want a connection that doesn't start with my kid. I like—" He pauses as his eyes trace the curves of my body, standing out in my tight jeans and shirt combo. "I like the fearlessness that comes with being you and how you've always had such huge goals. I like that you aren't afraid to speak your mind or tell me when I'm being too much. And I loved your hair. I always really loved your hair."

It's not lost on me that his speech changed from a general sense to a more personal one. My breathing comes quick, and I meet his eyes. His pupils are dilated and his irises seem almost darker. His face is just inches from mine.

"Oh," I breathe and move back. Poppy is absorbed by Rocket's soft fur and is now using him as a pillow. He doesn't seem to mind. But she's still here and I'm not about to get carried away in front of her and everyone else on this ranch. "Just to clarify . . ."

"I like you. And honestly, I liked you in high school too, but I know and understand why you didn't like me."

"Don't be ridiculous, Theo. Everyone had a crush on you in high school. Including me."

This unintentional admission shuts him up. He stares at me, confused, then breaks into a grin. I laugh breathily, embarrassed.

"I really thought you hated me."

"I wouldn't be here if I hated you."

Theo shrugs and I realize his hand still holds my wrist. "Well, you don't hate me now, but then. You never looked at me the same way after I fucked up your album project."

I lick my lips. While he's right, I don't think it matters anymore. I also didn't know he looked at me that closely to realize my opinion of him had changed. I'd spent high school believing I was invisible to everyone who wasn't in the nerdy, artsy crowd. I was wrong.

"And how am I looking at you now?"

He opens his mouth to answer and I'm certain if he leaned in to kiss me now that I would let him, but he doesn't get that far. Theo stiffens as the moms behind us begin to murmur and loud crying sounds out over the peaceful sounds of the ranch. I turn to find the group of girls and their horses heading back, Emma in front flanked by the instructors, tears running down her cheeks, clutching her left wrist to her chest.

"Oh fuck," Theo mutters, then he's on his feet.

I grab hold of Rocket's leash as Theo runs to his daughter.

Chapter Twelve

Theo takes Emma to the emergency room, his paramedic knowledge leading him to believe she's almost certainly broken her arm. I offer to take Rocket home so he doesn't have to worry about that. He easily hands over his house keys and texts me his address. As if on autopilot, I take Poppy back to my parents, then drop Rocket off at Theo's house. Miraculously, his house is only two streets away. Which I never knew and now wish I did much sooner. I have no idea how he afforded it considering how much houses go for around here, but I don't allow myself to dwell on it. Or I do, but not for long.

Instead, I find Rocket's food in the questionably green kitchen cabinets and sit with him until his whines subside. I pet him for over an hour, him pawing me whenever I dare to stop, then finally text Theo.

Magnolia: How is she?

Theo: The doctor just saw her. They generally don't like to make kids wait when they can help it, which is good! But I also may have connections that got us in sooner . . . They're taking her down for an X-ray shortly.

Magnolia: Do you need company?

※♩※

I hate hospitals. I haven't been in one since Iris died and Poppy came home. It's not as if I've refused to go to one if I needed it, but I haven't needed to in the last two years. Coming to the realization that I haven't been here since then fills me with an acute sense of dread. My chest constricts as I walk up to the emergency room doors. I try to even my breathing, especially since I already told Theo I'm here, and pray to the universe that I'm not about to hyperventilate or puke. I look up and breathe deeply. The *C* in Emergency has lost its colour and is now a pastel red compared to the vibrant reds next to it. Somehow this grounds me.

I walk through the doors and spot Theo hovering just behind the check-in desk. He plays the part of a worried parent well, and I don't know whether I should be disgusted that I'm attracted to him in this moment. How much he cares about his child is etched all over his skin. His posture is deflated, his brow is creased with worry, and he seems to be nervously playing with the bunched sleeves of his shirt just for something to do.

"Theo!" I call, loud enough so he can hear, but not so loud to disturb everyone else.

He waves a hand in response. I jog to catch up to him as he turns down the hallway towards Emma's temporary room. I've never been in this section of the hospital; luckily I'm not prone to emergency injuries in adulthood. The Oakville Trafalgar Memorial Hospital is almost ten years old now, but it still feels sleek and new. The emergency department is full of glass-fronted rooms instead of those classic curtained-off areas. Each room is separated by a solid wall. I'm just a little shocked to note how the layout keeps the area more open and airy.

Theo sinks down into a chair when we get back to Emma's room. Her horse-covered backpack lies at the bottom of the bed in her absence. There's no other chair, so I sit next to it. I point a foot and nudge Theo's leg, getting a smudge of mud on his jeans. He brushes it away and looks up at me with a pronounced sigh.

"I've been here over a thousand times for work, but you never get used to it when you're here for someone else, especially when it's your kid."

"Hey," I say, nudging him again, spreading the dirt. "She'll be fine. I broke my arm around her age too, and look." I hold my hands up and grin. "I'm fully functional now!"

He laughs and it eases the knots in my stomach. "Objectively, I know. A broken arm is one of the most common childhood injuries. In comparison to others, it doesn't take long to heal, and most kids aren't too mad about it because they get a cool colourful cast for people to sign. Emma's going to be fine, but this still sucks."

"I know."

"I just wish I could have stopped it from happening, you know? Cause now her confidence is going to be shaken. She's going to struggle to get back on the horse. Literally."

I chew on my bottom lip and look down at the floor where Theo's gaze is also trained. The knot in my stomach forms itself again as I relate to the potential struggles of a seven-year-old. I'm also struggling to get back on the horse and more so wondering if I even want to. I nearly tell him this, but stop myself. Another emotional woman is not what he needs right now.

"Tell me about Emma," I eventually say. He slowly brings his head up to face mine. A hesitant smile spreads across my face. "I'd love to know more about her."

Theo's posture relaxes and he leans back in his chair. He looks off into the distance dreamily, almost like a Disney princess imagining her future. I feel myself begin to fall for this man at the love he has for his daughter.

"You may have guessed I had her young," Theo says.

"Theo, I had no idea you were so talented and able to give birth to a child!"

He rolls his eyes and this time, he's the one to nudge me with his foot. He's the one to make me blush and not the other way around.

"I met this girl about a month before we graduated high school, and things got serious fast. She got pregnant pretty much right after we got together, but neither of us knew until about four months in. Which is . . . Does that make me look bad?"

I shrug. "It happens."

"Emma was born at the beginning of December, and she was two months premature. My girlfriend, uh, well, she left as soon as she could." He rubs the back of his neck and sighs deeply. "Emma spent about a month in the NICU, and her mother was nowhere to be found. She disconnected her phone. It was bad. The only way I was able to find out what happened to her was through her parents, who had pretty much disowned her after she abandoned us. I guess she realized she didn't want a child, so she just left. I haven't seen her since the day she gave birth. I try not to think about how Emma might feel about that someday . . . Like a cross-that-bridge when-we-get-there thing, you know?"

"Where does she think her mom is?"

"This might sound bad, but she's never asked. I'm all she's ever known. Well, me and my family. She also knows her mom's parents. I guess I should probably talk to her about it . . . I've just never really known how to bring up the subject."

"No, that's okay," I say quickly. "I can't imagine it would be an easy conversation, and it's certainly not one you have to think about now. I just wondered if she knew."

"She doesn't. Part of me wants to keep it that way for as long as possible. She is the furthest thing from unwanted, and I never want her to feel that way."

"I'm glad she has you."

His lips quirk momentarily, but I can tell just how much this weighs on him. The smile doesn't quite reach his eyes and he fidgets with his hands in his lap. I slide off the edge of the bed and reach out to him before I think to stop myself. I place my hand on his cheek, brushing my thumb against the stubble, causing him to look me in the eyes.

"I mean it. She's really lucky to have you," I say, though it comes out as more of a whisper.

His hand moves to the back of my neck, closing the inch gap between us. I've never kissed a man with a beard before, and I don't know if it's just because I really like Theo or if the beard really has an edge, but this might be the best kiss of my life. His lips are soft and skilled, matching the softness of his beard. His fingers knit themselves in the hair at the back of my neck that's fallen free from my messy ponytail. My world stops for a moment, and I'm done for. I'm falling for this man before I even decide I want to.

When he pulls back, there's a lazy smile on his face and I remember that we're in a hospital of all places. I definitely cannot go further than a simple kiss. I clear my throat and back away to my previous position on the bed. This makes him laugh, clearly in the same place I was.

I swallow a few times before I trust myself to speak properly. "What else?"

"Uhhh," he says, as if he's lost track of the conversation, but then he snaps back to it. "Right. Uh, Emma's the most intelligent little kid I know. She's really into science and animals. We volunteer at the Humane Society most weekends. I swear she's going to become a vet someday. I am really proud of that science drive, though, which may be my doing since I was also really into science as a kid."

"You know, I was always kind of surprised you were a science kid."

"That's mean."

"It is, and I'm sorry, but you can't tell me you never got that."

"No, I did. I mean, when you're just so damn attractive, everyone thinks you're—what's the word? Oh right, an idiot." I laugh, shoot him a tight smile, and slowly, politely extend my left arm to flip him off. He raises his eyebrows. "You know, I don't think I've ever been told to fuck off so nicely."

"I'm a woman of many talents. Go on."

"Did you know I wanted to be a doctor?"

"Surprisingly, yes I did." I scoot back far enough on the bed so I can dangle my legs and kick them over the edge. He follows my movement with his eyes. "I remember wondering why you were in an art class when all your other classes were science."

"Ah, that is because I *am* actually an idiot who forgot he needed an art credit until grade eleven."

"I thought they made you take one in grade nine."

"Usually, yes," he admits. "I had music in grade nine but dropped it after the third week because I messed up my shoulder playing hockey and that made it hard to play guitar."

"Man, an athletic musician who was going to be a doctor? Boy, you must have got all the girls."

"You keep saying that."

I shrug. "Old reputations die hard, I guess?"

"Do I have to kiss you again to make you think otherwise?" I flush and notice his ears are tinged pink again too. He smirks, then shakes his head. "For the record, I had sex once in high school and it wasn't until grade twelve."

"We have the same record, then."

We let this sit in the air between us for a moment. I don't know what assumptions he had about me before we started talking again, but I know this is new information to him. It's information maybe three people know other than me and my high school boyfriend. Theo's news, though, is interesting. I wonder how a rumour about him got so out of hand. I didn't know one girl at the school who didn't have some story about him, usually where he "loved and left" someone, but they were always secondhand stories. Maybe we really shouldn't have taken them at face value.

"Why aren't you a doctor?" I eventually ask.

He cocks his head. "Why aren't you a singer?" His words unintentionally sting me, just as much as they touch me that he remembers. "Life happened. I didn't want to spend the most important years of Emma's life killing myself on some degree. Maybe some people are able to do that. Maybe it's easier when you have two parents for one to go through medical school. I don't know. But I did what I had to do, and I kept my dream alive by becoming a paramedic. The dream just changed a bit."

I nod. "Life happens, all right."

He laughs. "Yeah, I figured you'd get that with Poppy."

Oh. There it is. If I didn't assume before, then I know now. He definitely thinks I'm Poppy's mom. "I'm actually not—"

Theo stands abruptly and grins as Emma is wheeled back into the room. She looks less than thrilled to be here, but her face lightens when she sees me. She looks between the two of us, then waves at me. I wave back.

"How're we doing?" Theo asks.

Chapter Thirteen

Theo steps out once Emma's cast has been fitted. He has to thank a buddy for getting Emma in so quickly. This leaves me alone with her for the first time. And considering that I've had one full conversation with her and am not quite sure where exactly I stand with her father, this makes me all kinds of nervous. Certainly more nervous than stepping onstage in front of a thousand people.

"How are you feeling?" I ask her. "Can I get you anything?"

Emma peers at me from her cross-legged perch on the hospital bed, and I suddenly feel as self-conscious as I did when I got ready this morning. I readjust myself in the chair Theo just vacated, pulling my ponytail over my left shoulder. I smile and try to make sure it's entirely genuine and not as awkward as I feel. Who knew a child could get me this on edge.

Emma doesn't answer my question. Instead, she launches into excitable speech.

"My dad likes you," she begins, as if this isn't a groundbreaking confession coming from the person who probably knows Theo best. "Like, really likes you. He keeps bringing you up all the time and I'm pretty sure he's just dropping hints and trying to see how I feel about you. But he's never talked about anyone around me before. I've never seen him like this. It's really weird, but I also think I kind of like it? Is that weird? I don't know you, but you seem nice and you're really pretty and Poppy is super cute too. Dad seems to like you guys and I want him to be happy, I guess. I invited you today."

I blink a few times, digesting her words before I realize I'm staring. I laugh awkwardly.

"Well, thank you, I think." I pause and note her fidgeting fingers sticking out of her purple cast. "Thank you for inviting me. You could have invited one of your friends, though."

She shakes her head. "No, I had to invite you so Dad would go out with you. He's been so worried about how I would feel that he wasn't going to ask."

"Wait . . . You made him ask me out?"

A small smile spreads across her face, followed by a giggle bubbling out. "I had to. I watched some old movie with my aunt a while ago where these kids got their parents back together, and Dad needed a nudge like that."

"Oh my God," I whisper. "You literally Parent Trapped me."

She shakes her head so hard it gives me whiplash. Just as I'm about to reach out to stop her head from snapping right off, she straightens. She looks at me with wide eyes, and I marvel at the clear split of clashing colours in her left eye.

"I'm not trying to make you my mom or anything," she says, a distinct edge in her voice that masks the flicker of hope in those wide eyes. "I just want my dad to be happy."

I don't push it any further. "How's your arm feeling?"

Emma returns my genuine but still kind of awkward smile from earlier. She holds up her arm and studies it with a grimace. I almost laugh, remembering my animosity when I first broke my arm.

"You know, I broke my arm when I was a kid," I say, and her drooped shoulders perk up. "Actually, I was exactly the same age as you."

"Really?"

"Mm-hmm. Yeah, I wasn't too happy about it at first, but when you go back to school it's a novelty and everyone wants a place to sign it."

"Will you sign mine?" she asks, batting her lashes as if I wasn't already planning to autograph her cast. "How did you break yours?"

I dig around in my purse, searching for some kind of writing utensil while I speak. "Long story short, I was in a talent show and a kid pushed me off the stage."

Her mouth drops open. "And you got back on? My dad said you're a singer, so clearly you got back on the stage again. But I just wouldn't if that happened."

My hands pause in my bag. I can see Theo's fears about Emma leaving horseback riding playing out on her face, and it breaks my heart a little bit. But just as my heart breaks for the potential shattering of any dreams she has, it breaks for the fact that I haven't stood on a stage aside from a shitty karaoke one in two years. When it really mattered, I didn't get back on.

I swallow. "Yeah, I went back. It was something . . . Uh, it was something I really loved. My sister was also a huge support. She made sure I didn't give up based on someone else's mistake."

Emma chews her lip and I debate whether that was the right thing to say. I don't know kids this age well enough to know if she'll focus on my use of the past tense or if she'll zero in on it being someone else's mistake. I don't know how she fell, but I've known equestrians who take their failures very seriously.

I gesture toward her backpack, and she looks down. "Got any markers in there?"

She unfolds her legs and pulls her bag onto her lap. It doesn't take her long to find her similarly horse-decorated pencil case. She unzips it and hands me a gold Sharpie. I take it from her appreciatively.

"Fabulous colour choice," I say. "Where do you want my autograph?"

She points to a spot on the inside of her wrist and holds her arm out for me. I gingerly take it in my hand and sign my name. Then, just like Iris and I always used to do, I draw a flower next to it. Emma steals her arm back and runs her fingers over the script.

"Do you always go by Magnolia? Or do you have a nickname?" she asks and meets my eyes.

I sit next to her on the bed, mattress crinkling beneath me. "Magnolia is fine. I think it's nice because it's different. I've never met another. But it is a long name and sometimes it's easier to just say Lia. That's been my nickname for, like, twenty years. I've also gotten Mags once or twice."

"Mags like *The Hunger Games*?" Theo asks, choosing this moment to reappear. "I like it."

I raise my eyebrows and stand. Theo winks at me then

takes my place next to Emma. I hand him the gold marker. "Your turn to sign, Theodore."

Chapter Fourteen

Hanna licks her fingers after devouring the last onion ring. I plop down next to her, tired and just the slightest bit overwhelmed, and set a timer on my phone for when this round of speed dating is up. I watch from the booth nearest to the front where several rows of tables are set up specifically for singles to mingle, and think about my current journey into maybe-not-singlehood.

"You have to stop inviting me here after work," Hanna says and reaches for a loaded cheesy nacho. "I have no self-control after a long shift."

"Isn't every day a long shift?" I mutter and shove chips into my mouth.

"Yes," she answers with certainty, then pauses my hand mid-chip grab. "Slow down and talk to me. Why are you freaking out? You guys are basically dating now, right? And from everything you've said, he's a really nice guy. What's the issue? Do I have to meet him and judge him for you?"

"I think I'm judgemental enough for the both of us," I say with a laugh and crunch the chip she stopped me from eating.

"So then . . ." she says, motioning for me to get on with it. "Girl, why did you SOS me here on a Wednesday night, four days after your date?"

"It wasn't a date."

"No, but it was a kiss."

My phone timer barks. Hanna holds back a laugh. The alarm on my phone has been a dog barking since the day I got a phone when I was fourteen. I slip out of the leather-padded booth and step in front of the mic on the mirror stage.

"All right, singles!" I announce. The group looks up, several relieved, some indifferent, and a select few disappointed. "It's time to switch up for the final speed date of the night! Switch to your left one last time. I'm crossing my fingers for a match for y'all!" I wait for everyone to switch, then settle. "And go!"

Hanna stares at me patiently from her place at the booth, hands folded in front of her. I have half a mind to walk away, but I invited her here. I SOSed her here. And despite how I no longer feel very SOS-y and only momentarily freaked out, I still have to talk to her.

"So," she says as I sit down, casually sipping from her glass of water with a straw. "What's happening?"

I place my phone on the table and watch the speed dating seconds tick away. To Hanna's credit, she doesn't pry. She just sits, blowing bubbles with her straw. I switch my gaze from my timer app to her stormy water. With a deep breath, I finally admit what's on my mind.

"I like him, like, a lot. And according to Emma, he feels the same about me. And I know I could probably fall for him, and I'm pretty sure that's what his daughter is rooting for, and I haven't felt like this in a long time, and he just makes me feel really good about myself. He asked me out, like formally."

Hanna blinks a few times, digesting my ramble. "Okay, so you both like each other and he asked you on a date. That's what we're dealing with?"

"When you say it like that, my freak-out sounds really stupid."

"No, not stupid. Maybe an overreaction, but not stupid. I don't think you're freaking out negatively, either. You're excited as much as you are scared. That's totally normal."

I shrug. "Yeah, I guess."

Though I can't remember a time when I've been this freaked out over dating someone. Every time I'm around Theo, my stomach explodes in butterflies. He makes my skin feel like it's on fire every time he touches me. He makes my cheeks burn, and no doubt he could probably make me burn with desire. I want him more than I've wanted any other guy I've been with. So why the hesitation?

"Go for it," Hanna says as my dog barks. "I said it to you last time I was here and I'm saying it again. You deserve to have someone hype you up. You deserve to move forward in your life."

I swallow and slide out of the booth. I stumble onto the stage and accidentally clear my throat into the mic.

"Sorry," I mumble, then put on my stage voice. "That's all for tonight, folks! I hope you've found yourself interested in someone, but if not, come back for more speed dating next month! And if you do come back in October, remember to wear a costume because it's Halloween speed dating! Thanks so much for coming. If you're interested in more of our events, we have our monthly Thursday-night trivia tomorrow and karaoke every Tuesday!"

I return the mic to its stand and blink in surprise when Zac turns the spot off. The stage goes dim, unreflective, and takes on a sepia tone. I pack away the sign-up sheet for this week and watch a few couples form. I want to be able to allow myself that. The easy way they're smiling at each other and that connection you can feel right off the bat.

I close my eyes, take a breath, and picture nothing other than Theo in my mind.

"Okay, I actually have to work now," I say to Hanna, leaning against her booth.

"No worries," she says and pulls some money out of her wallet. "I have to head out anyway, but remember what I said, okay?"

"I know you're right. Doesn't make it any less terrifying to jump into something with him."

"Well, Lia, I like him. Outside of thinking he was cute in high school, I think he's a good guy and you should go for it. Everything you've told me sounds good, and I trust your judgement. You've never had a shitty ex, just exes that weren't right for you. Theo might be the right one. You never know, you just have to try. When's the date?"

I push a table back to its original spot, just to look busy, as Hanna gets ready to go.

"Not sure yet. Maybe this weekend? Trivia night is the last day I work this week, so I guess if things line up then that'll be it."

Hanna nods and points her keys at me. "Okay, I'm holding you to it. Call me if you need help with an outfit or a pep talk or something."

I smile and nod, but vow to myself that I won't need her. I'll pull the old confident Magnolia out of the recesses of my mind and get on with life.

Chapter Fifteen

I'm still grumbling to myself as I pull into the parking lot of Munn's Public School where my mom works. Her car broke down this morning on her way to school, so she got it towed away and according to her, is now stranded at work without a way home, even though we live in this school district about six streets away. She could have walked.

Even so, I park the Bug by the side door and sit. Poppy sleeps in the back, annoyed I woke her from her afternoon nap, but making the most of it in her car seat. I text my mom that I'm here, just the slightest bit before the bell, then lean my head back against the headrest and close my eyes.

It's been one of those really long toddler days. Poppy is sprouting some new teeth. The internet tells me molars are bitches to come in, and I definitely believe it. Poppy's alternated between being extremely clingy and extremely devious all day. The whiplash is making me lose my mind but so is the drawing on the walls, knocking every book off her little shelf, and climbing anything remotely climbable. This nap I had to interrupt is the only break I've had today.

My eyes snap open as someone knocks at my window.

My heart pounds in my chest for no good reason because obviously I'm not going to die in a crowded, primarily child-based parking lot, but I was still out of it enough to not take in my surroundings. I roll down the window, seeing only a man's broad chest through it.

"Hey," Theo says, poking his head through my window, a goofy grin on his face. "Fancy seeing you here."

"I had to pick up my mom," I explain. "Emma goes to school here?"

"Yeah. You know where I live. It was the easiest place for school. She can walk to or from if I'm working, but I do try to pick her up."

I smile. "That's really sweet of you to make the effort." And then, because all the pieces fall together and I'm unsure whether it's a good thing, I say with certainty, "My mom is Emma's teacher."

His eyes widen slightly, but only for a moment. "I feel like an idiot for not putting that together. Yeah, Mrs. Callas. Emma loves her, if that makes you less mortified."

"Oh, good, I'm that transparent."

"We should play poker sometime," he jokes. "I'm glad I ran into you, though. Are you busy tonight?"

I sigh. "I work tonight."

"Oh. Okay, never mind." I don't know how to feel about the joy that rips through me at his disappointment. "How about Saturday?"

"Saturday works."

Usually, I love trivia night. It's fun picking out vaguely obscure questions and getting hyped up in the atmosphere, but today, I'm not feeling it. If I'm being honest, I haven't been feeling the pub life for a while, it's just become more obvious the more I hang around Theo. When I'm with him, I feel lighter than I have for two years. I feel like that girl with the wealth of potential all over again.

So, standing on some stage with hot spotlights illuminating me, not singing feels wrong somehow.

"Do we have any Canadian history buffs in here?" I ask, raising my hand and cheering when two other people raise their hands right along with me. "This one's for you! Who was Canada's first French-speaking prime minister?"

I wait a bit as my loyal subjects conference with each other. The history buffs look on confidently while the other teams scramble. This question is Hanna's doing. Hanna, whose last name is Laurier, with no connection to the former PM. Hanna, who chose to go to Wilfred Laurier University solely because their last names were the same.

"Shoutout to my best friend for that question!" I say and lift the champagne flute in the air. A couple who frequents our trivia nights had gotten engaged tonight in the pub, so we toasted. "Next question! For all the Swifties out there. How long is the extended version of 'All Too Well'? I will give you bonus points if you get it down to the second, but I'm just looking for the round number."

Chatter begins again as tables try to figure out how to gain these bonus points. This is the energy I typically love, but today my smile doesn't reach my eyes. That is, until the bell above the front door jingles and someone walks in. As if I'm in a movie, my eyes are immediately drawn to the door, never mind the fact that people come and go regularly and I never take notice. And it's not like I believe in the cosmic power of the universe that draws two people together as soulmates, but it feels like the cosmic power of the universe is drawing me towards my soulmate when I make eye contact with Theo the second he walks into the pub. He finds me right away as well, and I suddenly feel like we're eye fucking each other in this crowd of strangers.

"Uhh," I stutter out, then force myself to look down at my trivia questions. I scan the list until I find my place, then accidentally read out the same question. "My bad. That is not the next question."

Once my face is no longer cherry-red and I've announced the trivia winners, I tell Andy I'm taking my break. He doesn't argue with me, just waves me off into the oblivion of a free half hour. I hang my apron up on its hook and pull my hair out of its ponytail. My waves are a little frizzy, because that's life in a hot kitchen and under stage lights, but they're otherwise looking pretty bouncy and shiny, so it's an overall win. I thank the outfit gods that I decided to wear a leather mini skirt tonight, one that hugs my curves and sucks me in just enough. A far better look than my standard frazzled Poppy vibe.

I scan the pub from behind the bar and once more, find him easily. Theo sits next to the sequin stage at one of the only empty tables. A beer sits in front of him, a menu just under his nose. He concentrates on our very greasy options as if his life depends on this choice. I smile and slip out from behind the bar.

"Can I take your order, sweet cheeks?" I say with a southern twang as I slip into the chair opposite him.

Theo looks up, already laughing. "What do you recommend? Completely serious."

"What level of grease do you enjoy?"

"The maximum."

"We have really great burgers."

"Oh," he says and shakes his head. "Well, not that. I should have said no meat."

I raise my eyebrows. "You're a vegetarian?"

"Emma is, so I try to keep to it. She wants to go full-on vegan, but I'm drawing the line at no meat for now. I can't give up cheese."

I laugh and agree with him. Cheese reigns supreme on the food scale.

"Okay, then how about mozza sticks?"

"Only if you join me."

"Look, I'm a slut for mozza sticks. You don't have to ask me twice. Plus, I'm on break."

I glance around the pub, trying to find someone who works here. I catch Chloe's eye and wave her over, but she either doesn't see me or ignores me, because she turns away. I shrug it off as Zac walks up to our table. We get the mozza sticks and Zac ribs me for sleeping on the job.

So be it.

Theo takes a sip of his beer and drinks me in. "So how do you do it?"

"Do what?"

"When do you sleep?" he asks with a laugh. "I remember toddlers. They're up at the crack of dawn and just keep going all day."

I open my mouth to explain my situation but pause. He's not entirely wrong, even though I'm not Poppy's mother. I get home from the pub and go to sleep, praying that Poppy doesn't wake up at 6:00 a.m. or that I can convince her to stay in bed with me for a few hours. Sometimes I win, sometimes I'm a background actor in *The Walking Dead*.

"Okay, so first, I don't know," I say and I know he gets it. He reaches out to me and holds my hand. "But I just have to clarify something. Poppy . . . Poppy isn't mine."

His face falls and confusion overtakes his bushy eyebrows. "What do you mean?"

"I'm not Poppy's mother. She's my sister's kid. I guess I'm, like, the nanny or something. I spend the day with Poppy while my parents work and then I come here."

He's silent for a moment and I try to pull my hand away, thinking this omission is a dealbreaker. That I've somehow proven myself as a liar and I don't deserve to hang around with him or his daughter again. But as I slip away from his grip, he locks his fingers around mine. I look up from the scuffed and stained wood of the table and into his eyes. There's confusion there, yes, but they're soft and open and nothing has changed in them.

"That doesn't seem fair to you," he says finally, and I let out a breathy laugh that doesn't sound like me. "Where's Iris? What is she doing that she can't be around her daughter?"

I close my eyes, both at the mention of her name and the implication. My admission hurts him because he thinks Iris is doing the same thing as Emma's mother. But if Iris had any control over the end of her story, she never would have left Poppy. When I open my eyes, I'm shocked to find the world is blurry. I blink away the tears before they fall, but I feel the avalanche building, similar to how I broke down the day after she died.

"She's dead," I whisper, though it's so quiet that in the buzz of the pub, I'm not sure he even heard me.

But every inch of him freezes. "I'm sorry, did you just

say she's dead?" I don't trust myself to speak, so I just nod. "God, Magnolia, I'm so sorry. How long ago was this?"

"It'll be two years in December," I say.

I can't meet his eyes. I know the depth of emotion I'll see there, and I can't risk looking up and falling to pieces. It's bad enough that he's the only one to have mentioned her name or even really asked about her in over a year. It's like she never existed in the places she so vividly brought to life. But here is this man, willing to bring her back, and he doesn't even know how deeply that touches me.

"Wow," he breathes and squeezes my hand. "Did she . . . Was it childbirth that . . ."

I swallow the lump in my throat, but it doesn't go away, so my voice comes out gruff with emotion. "She contracted a blood infection and died a few days after Poppy was born."

A tear slides down my cheek and I wipe it away with the back of my hand. At this moment, I realize I've never had to say that to anyone. Everyone in my life just knew what happened to her and everyone who didn't never asked, as if it was too taboo to know. My heart drops into my stomach, then further, until it feels like it's not even part of my body anymore.

"That's terrible. She would have been, what, twenty-five?" I nod. "Did she at least get to meet Poppy?" Another nod. I shield my face with my hair as more tears spill over the edges of my eyelashes. Theo squeezes my hand again, then places his other hand overtop our joined ones. "Do you want to talk about something else? I'm sorry. I didn't mean to make you cry. I just had no idea."

"No," I say and surprise myself. "It's good. No one ever fucking talks about her, and I miss her so damn much."

"I didn't know her well, or really at all, but I remember you guys were always together."

"She was my best friend." That same breathy laugh bursts out of me again.

I place my hand against my chest as it constricts. My breath comes fast and in bursts between sobs that I don't quite understand because I'm not crying hard enough for that. The noise in the pub dulls around me as I make these tiny gasps for breath. My heart returns to my body and slams against my ribcage. It pounds in my ears, making it hard to focus on anything other than my damn heartbeat and the fact that there is not enough air in my body. I can't breathe.

I jump violently as the plate of mozzarella sticks appears on the table between me and Theo. The shock of noise, an actual noise and not just the ringing of my ears, stutters air into my lungs and I cough. Theo has a muffled conversation with who I can only assume is Zac, but I'm not sure why it's muffled because I'm right here. But all I can hear, all I can sense is a dull roar.

And then I'm on my feet, somehow, and out into the cool autumn air. I feel a wall behind me and slide down it.

"It's okay. I'm here. You're okay."

Theo. I focus on his voice as he repeats these comforting phrases over and over again. At some point, he must have settled down next to me; his arm wraps around my shoulders, pulling my body into his.

"You're okay. Just breathe through it."

His body heat against mine does something to me, and I feel myself start to even out again. The sobs lessen considerably, vision refocuses, though it's still hazy through tears. My breathing normalizes to the point that

I'm able to take a deep breath and fill my lungs. After about a minute of silence, Theo's hand comes below my chin, and I turn to him.

"Are you all right?" Theo asks. "Have you had a panic attack before?"

I let out a puff of air and shake my head. "That would be a first."

"Glad to guide you through," he says and salutes me.

I laugh, and though it's wet, it's not the same injured one that kept escaping my body inside.

"Thank you," I whisper and lick my lips.

I lean into him and close my eyes. That couldn't have been more than ten minutes of my life, but I'm exhausted. My body feels as though it's run a marathon, and I guess as far as emotions go, it kind of has.

"You don't have to go back in," Theo says and I startle. I begin to question him and he continues, "The waiter, Zac?" I nod. "I talked to him and another waitress came over. They saw you weren't exactly yourself and said they'd cover for you. Seems you don't call out much, so they didn't think it'd be a problem."

"I never call out," I breathe, suddenly embarrassed by this fact, and that two other people saw me sobbing in the middle of a crowded restaurant.

"Can I take you home? I don't know if you feel up to driving, but I'd recommend not driving, if possible."

"Is that your official medical advice?"

"It might be."

"Can I come home with you?"

Chapter Sixteen

Rocket lunges at me as I walk through the front door of Theo's house. Once more, he catches me off balance, but I don't mind when I fall back into Theo's chest. His hands clamp down on my elbows, then move down my body until they're settled on my hips. I shimmy out of his grasp and bend down to pet the dog.

"I see you have a wing man," I say, with a smirk directed at him over my shoulder.

Theo shrugs and steps around me after discarding his shoes on the front mat. "He's cuter than me, so I can't win."

I laugh and sit down on the cool linoleum of the small foyer. The cold seeps through my bare legs and I shiver. Rocket bonds to me. He sits squarely in the centre of my lap, as if he's a lap dog and not a fully grown Bernese. I'm not one to know how a panic attack feels, or how it feels in the moments after, but as I hold on to this mass of fur, drool, and love, my nerves calm. I bury my face in his fur and breathe him in like I would Poppy's baby-powder skin.

"Hey, you don't have to sit on the floor," Theo says, peeking out from his green kitchen. He snaps his fingers, calling Rocket to attention. "Rocket, come!"

Rocket licks my hand, then trots off to the kitchen. I pick myself off the floor and pad away to meet him.

"You stole my dog," I say.

Theo smirks at me as I turn the corner. He stands next to a sparkly pink kettle, two mugs next to it on the speckled laminate countertop. I lean against the island just behind him and fold my arms over my chest.

"Your dog? I think you stole him from me."

Rocket settles on top of my feet and I smile triumphantly. Theo pours hot water into the mugs and stirs them. He opens the fridge and pulls out a can of whipped cream and chocolate sauce, then decorates the top of each mug.

"It's not my fault if he likes me more than you."

"He's an attention whore," Theo says and turns to face me, unicorn mug of hot chocolate in hand. I take it from him and he picks up a University of Toronto mug for himself. "He'll follow anyone new and anyone who'll feed him. Won't you, boy?"

Rocket thumps his tail loudly against the tiled floor. I take a sip of the hot chocolate as I glance around the kitchen for the second time this week, but this time with an audience.

"Why does your kitchen look like the eighties?"

"Why does the whole house look like the eighties is a better question." Theo smirks behind his mug. "My parents downsized two years ago. This was their second home after they got married. I grew up here with my siblings, and then Emma came along. They sold me the house when they moved. Told me it's Emma's home now too and I shouldn't have to uproot her life just because they were leaving. I would have found an apartment or something, but this . . . Well, this was . . . I couldn't pass it up."

I shake my head, move my feet enough that Rocket displaces himself, and advance into the family room. It's the one room on the main floor that's firmly rooted in 2023.

"I wouldn't pass it up either."

Theo follows my footsteps. The family room is well lit, open concept, and bleeds in from the kitchen. The couch that I'd hung out with Rocket on last Saturday is a plush black leather and complements the deep burgundy walls. I love the cozy feel; the couch and chairs arranged in a circle around the room; the television mounted on the wall, surrounded by bookshelves; the double doors leading out to trees and a smattering of leaves covering the vast grass of the backyard. I could imagine myself cozying up in one of the armchairs with a similarly decadent hot chocolate, looking out at falling snow.

I ease myself down onto the centre of the couch. "I love this room."

"Thank you," Theo says. He sits next to me, placing his hot chocolate on the coffee table in front of us. I follow suit, then let him pull me to him. "This room is entirely my doing. It's the first I've redone down here. Slowly, but steadily making it our own."

"What else have you done?"

"Emma's room was first. She got my sister's room after my sister moved out, which was the year after Emma was born. My sister moved when she was twenty-three, so it was not a kid's room at the time and the second I was able to change it, I did. Then, I redid the master—what used to be my parents' room but is now mine."

"I imagine you wanted something a bit different."

He nods with a bit of a laugh. "Something that hadn't been their marriage bed for forty years, yeah."

"Definitely something that would need a bit of a switch up," I say with the slightest cringe, imagining starting my life in my parents' bedroom. "What's the next project?"

"The basement, I think. Kind of a random choice, but I actually like the ugly country kitchen."

"Oh, Theo, no!" I laugh harder than intended and I only realize why after I've stopped. "Sorry. Iris and I had a joke about kitchens like this. The ugly geese people have in them . . . you have one just hanging there on your puke-green backsplash."

"You know, I don't think that's how they sell that particular colour, but you should let the paint salesmen know."

He pulls me closer, and I tuck my legs up underneath me. I don't think about how we haven't talked about what we are. I don't think about how he just saw me at my lowest. I don't think about how I haven't even truly known him that long. I just let myself relax into him and feel safe. I think about how good it feels to be in his arms. I let myself live without questioning whether I deserve it for the first time in almost two years.

"Where's Emma?" I ask.

"Friend's house. Sleepover."

"On a school night? You're not just a regular dad, are you? You're a Cool Dad."

Theo laughs and I hear it through his chest with my head against him. I smile, unabashed, knowing he can't see it. Though I think I'd smile for him anyway. We breathe each other in in silence for a long stretch of time. I don't know how long it lasts, only that it's not uncomfortable. It's the best silence has felt in years. I look up at him and find his eyes already on me. He opens his mouth to speak, but I close the gap and kiss him. His hand comes below my chin and cradles my jawline, tipping my head just right for this angle. I bring my hands up to feel his hair, something I've been wanting to do since, well, since I was sixteen. Nearly ten years later, it's so incredibly gratifying. His hair is soft, well kept, perfect to tangle up in, just like his lips.

I pull back and bite the smile overtaking my features. Theo's face, I'm sure, matches my own. His cheeks are flushed and he's grinning. His pupils dilate once more and I fucking love the way he looks at me. Like I belong here. Like I'm a part of his home. Like he wants me. And good God, I want him.

"Theo," I whisper. "Thank you."

"For what?"

I swallow and let out everything I'm feeling. "For helping me through that at the pub and knowing exactly what to do, getting me somewhere safe, then giving me hot chocolate and a dog to calm me down. For, honestly, just being yourself and being so kind to me over the past few weeks. For looking at me like I'm the most beautiful woman on the planet. But mostly, for letting me talk about Iris."

"I don't know why you wouldn't talk about her," he says, his thumb absently stroking along my cheekbone. "She's such a huge part of you and that doesn't change because she died. She's still your sister. She still existed."

I nod and find myself tearing up again. "She is. She's always going to be my sister and I don't want to forget that like other people seem so ready to do."

A tear falls from my eye and Theo brushes it away. He kisses me, slowly, softly. I melt into him.

"Tell me about her," he whispers against my lips.

So I do. I tell him all about Iris until we both fall asleep.

Chapter Seventeen

I wake with a crick in my neck and a very stuffed nose. My eyes adjust to bright sunlight streaming in through the glass doors and my brain stutters, remembering I'm not at home. I'm lying on a couch, my head on Theo's chest, sandwiched between him and the back cushions.

"Good morning," Theo says, running a hand through my messy hair.

"Morning," I say.

"I hate to cut this moment short, but I have to go to work."

I clumsily try to push myself up, which only causes him to fall to the floor at the unexpected movement. I apologize between frenzied laughter as Rocket rushes up to Theo and licks every inch of his face. As I move to sit up, Theo grasps my ankle and pulls me down on top of him. I land squarely on his stomach and push the air out of his lungs. Rocket barks and climbs over Theo to get to me. My body shakes with unbidden giggles as I plant myself firmly on the floor and Rocket plants himself in my lap. Theo sits up with a grunt.

"That totally backfired."

"I'm so sorry," I say, but it comes out shaky through my laughter. At the sheer joy on my face, Theo joins in. When I catch my breath, I place my hand on his chest. "You should go."

"I should," he says, but he kisses me instead.

It's not long. It's nothing crazy. But it tells me everything he's thinking and everything he's left unsaid this morning.

"Thank you for letting me know about Iris," he says, hand trailing along my jawline, eyes boring into mine. "There are mozzarella sticks in the fridge if you want them."

I laugh. "You took the sticks?"

"Of course."

Theo drops me off at the pub so I can grab the Bug and head home. It's at this point, in front of our garage, that I finally check my phone. I've missed calls and texts from my parents, and a few from Chloe and Hanna, who say they want to have lunch with me today. I text off a quick *sure*, then step out of my car. The garage door opens.

"Hey, Bug," my dad says when he sees me. I don't know when the nickname started, but it stuck. It's part of the reason Iris got the Bug in the first place.

"Hey, Dad. How's Mom?"

He chuckles. "Well, I can't say she's too happy right now. I do believe she's about to call the police to report you missing."

"It hasn't even been twenty-four hours. How disappointing," I quip and make my way into the garage.

I throw my arms around his neck to hug him. "I love you, Dad."

My candour shocks him and it takes him a few seconds to wrap his arms around me too. We stay like that for a minute, just breathing. It feels so normal. Like the old us before Iris died and an invisible wedge was driven through the love this family once freely exuded.

"What was that about?" Dad asks as I pull away.

I shrug. "I don't know. Just had a bad night and need everyone to know that I love them."

He frowns and straightens his lilac-dotted tie. "I know that, Bug. And I love you too." He turns to his car, then pauses. "Are you all right? You said you had a bad night, and you didn't make it home until now. What's up?"

I think about how to best approach what's going on in my life, all my hesitation and re-ignition. How I had my first ever panic attack and it was ridiculously unpleasant but made me see things a different way—made me see how stilted my life has become because I haven't been able to process the past two years. How badly I want to remember Iris in this house. How I've fallen for a guy in a matter of weeks because he listens to me and looks at me and makes me feel seen. But I'm a mess and I don't know where to begin. Dad waits patiently, as always, leaning against the door of his car as I try to decipher my night.

And I wind up smiling, instead. "You know, it wasn't that bad. It started out that way, but I think I'm okay."

Dad nods. He purses his lips and makes a similar frozen face to my own, trying to figure out his next words. "So, I need to meet this boy."

"What makes you think there's a boy?" I ask, though I'm sure the heat creeping up my neck gives me away.

"I know you." He touches his nose, then opens the door to the flower van and slides in. "I do need to meet him. I promise I won't judge him too hard."

I laugh as I squeeze past the flower-mobile and up the garage steps. Poppy greets me when I open the door with one of her classic, crinkle-nosed smiles. I won't be going back to sleep today, much as I probably should since I stayed up most of the night talking, but somehow I don't feel tired. I gather Poppy into my arms and spin her around.

"What are we going to do today, Pops? Should we go out for a fancy tea party lunch with Hanna?"

Poppy adores Hanna. Like, follows her around and insists to be held by her 24/7 whenever she comes over kind of love. They have impassioned conversations in Poppy's garbled English.

My mom bustles into the room, worry creasing every line of her face, and I hold back a sigh.

"Where have you been?" she screeches, then pulls me tight against her chest. The air rips out of my lungs for a hot minute.

"I just slept over at a friend's place and forgot to call," I say when I can breathe again. "Besides, I'm twenty-five. You don't have to keep constant tabs on me."

She narrows her eyes at me and shakes her head. "You live under my roof. I'll be keeping tabs on you until you can keep them on yourself."

"And when exactly is that? I'm your live-in nanny, remember? I can't leave until you let me go."

My sudden burst of anger shocks me and I let Poppy loose on the ground. She runs off as Mom fixes me with a glare. I return her stare, levelled, realizing how much the assumption that I'll take care of Poppy bugs me. There has been so much unspoken since Iris's death.

"No one ever told you to do that, honey. If you don't want to take care of her, don't."

"Look, you know how much I love Poppy, but you also must know this wasn't my choice. I never volunteered to take care of her. I got back from my trip and basically had a baby thrusted at me. You decided you had to go back to work and didn't give me the choice to go back to what I loved."

Mom sighs, defeated. She lowers her eyes and picks her rainbow-studded work bag off the floor. "If you really loved it, you'd go back."

I watch her pass me, too stunned to come up with a comeback or anything else to say. The sentiment doesn't shock me. Of course she'd believe I don't love my singing enough to go back to it. She convinced herself it wasn't a viable career for so long. What shocks me is how flippant she is. How she thinks this was my choice when a week after I got home, she went back to work and I was suddenly a nanny. I remember sitting down at the table, talking about the next steps with Poppy, not even realizing they'd already made up their minds until the conversation was over. For months, I did nothing but raise Poppy while my parents worked. I made no money, wrote no songs, saw no one other than my family.

I didn't choose this, and now I don't know how to get out. Especially when my only conversation results in the exact same thing: my mother leaving to go to work while I stay with Poppy.

"Where are you, Pops?" I call and wipe away a tear. I

find her in the kitchen, raiding the cereal cabinet, dumping Cheerios on the floor. "Of course."

❃♪❃

The morning passes in a blur and soon Poppy and I sit at a booth inside Mo's Family Restaurant. She watches the passing cars from our window seat with interest and, to my surprise, patiently waits for Hanna while scratching the wooden window frame. Chloe arrives first, which disappoints Poppy. I laugh at her pout and bribe her with the promise of chicken fingers.

"Are you okay?" Chloe asks the second she sits down.

"Were you the other waitress who saw me last night?" I ask, and her confused stare tells me the answer before she does.

"What? No. I just heard you went home after trivia. Zac seemed a little worried for you. Said you went home with this guy he'd never seen before."

"I promise you, I'm fine," I say.

And now I realize this is not a Fun Lunch. This is a Reassurance Lunch.

Poppy squeals and fights to crawl over me and out of our booth as Hanna walks around the corner and joins our table. I shimmy out of the booth and allow Hanna to take my seat next to Poppy. I settle in next to Chloe instead.

"There's my favourite girl!" Hanna announces. Poppy reaches her arms out and Hanna leans over to kiss her little forehead, then she turns to me. "All right. How are you? I hear you had a panic attack last night, and that doesn't sound like you at all."

"How do you know that?" I ask.

Hanna blushes. "A little birdie told me. Theo messaged

me on Facebook."

"What?" I'm not entirely sure how I feel about that. Whether I'm flattered or a little annoyed.

"It wasn't anything bad. And he only messaged me. He just wanted someone who knows you well to check up on you. Make sure you were okay. Honestly, I think that's really sweet."

I let my gaze drift to the menu so that I don't gush about him, much as I want to. I don't really want this lunch to be the Magnolia Show, even though I know that's why they both wanted to meet up.

"Did you spend the night?" Chloe asks.

"I slept over," I say and eye Poppy, who is content to play with Hanna's fingers. "I did not sleep with him."

"So he didn't take advantage of you when you were vulnerable? That's what we were worried about at UFO. This guy we've never seen drives off with you while you're crying, and it just seems very weird. Like, we all know a guy who gets a little more from a girl when she's like that, you know? It was the gossip last night."

"Oh, great," I mumble. "I love being pub gossip. But, wait, if you were worried, why did you let me go with him?"

Chloe shrugs and plucks the drink menu from the centre of the table. "I dunno. Ask Zac."

I let the conversation die there, at least for the time being. It doesn't matter what Chloe and the pub think. I know what happened last night, and I know I would have been lost in my emotions without his guidance. A waitress comes over to take our orders. Poppy pulls out her cute act and whispers, "Chicken fingers" while blinking her blonde lashes at the waitress. We each order something different: Hanna a cheese omelette with hash browns and toast, Chloe a decadent grilled cheese, and me chocolate chip pancakes.

Hanna studies me from across the table as she has a whispered conversation with Poppy. When she can't keep her thoughts to herself any longer, she hands Poppy the crayon she was absently doodling with and speaks.

"I just want to say that I never knew how to act after Iris died."

"Oh," I say, caught off guard. "So he told you that much?"

"Just that you guys were talking about Iris. And that surprised me because you never do."

"No one ever does. I was just taking their lead. Talking about her last night felt amazing. After that initial burst of anxiety, I felt so much lighter. I've held so much in about her and I don't think I want to anymore."

"Okay, good to know," Hanna says, smile bright. "So we'll talk about her, then. Whenever you want. I hate that too. There have been so many things that've reminded me of her over the past two years that I've wanted to say, but I never knew if it was my place because no one else mentioned it. Like Poppy, when she thinks something is gross so she makes that face where she sticks out her tongue and kind of gags a bit."

I laugh. "Oh God, that's Iris."

Hanna's eyes shine, almost like she's on the verge of tears, and she might be. It's how I felt last night as well, she just doesn't have the same overwhelming sense of panic that came with letting the floodgates open.

"Seriously, whenever you need to talk about her, just go

for it. I thought it bothered you to mention her, but now I see I was wrong. I'm glad Theo was there for you." I smile and nod. I am too. Hanna lifts her glass of lemonade. "To Iris!"

I raise my glass and, after a moment, Chloe does as well. Poppy, not one to be left out, raises her sippy cup full of milk. I meet her eyes, and though she doesn't know the gravity of the situation, I'm so glad to have this little slice of Iris here as we toast to her.

"To Iris!"

Chapter Eighteen

The next week passes with me and Theo texting constantly. Our work schedules don't line up most of the time, with him working twelve-hour days and me going from Poppy time to pub time. We take to "accidentally" running into each other at school pickup or the grocery store. Poppy always claps when she spots her apple friend.

I still haven't officially told my parents about him. Not because I don't want to, but because I don't want to jinx anything before we have a chance to go on an official date. Stolen kisses and sneaky midnight phone calls on the way home are fun, but they're not a whole evening together.

Theo: What are you doing for Thanksgiving?

> **Magnolia:** The usual. Having dinner with the fam

Theo: Oh. So you're busy?

> **Magnolia:** I don't have to be . . . Why?

My phone rings at the dinner table, Theo's name and number on display. I'm thankful I haven't changed his contact photo yet. Both my parents snap their eyes to me immediately. I'm sure they noticed me texting beneath the table, but this is a bit more forward than a text.

"I'm just going to . . . I'll be right back," I say and stumble out of my chair as I excuse myself. As I climb the stairs, I answer him. "Hey!"

"Hey, so I was thinking . . ." Theo says.

I close my bedroom door, lean against it, and laugh. "That's dangerous."

"Shut up," he says, and Emma says something in the background. I can't quite make it out, but it sounds like she's asking about the phone call. "I was wondering if you wanted to spend Thanksgiving with me and my family."

I suck in a sharp breath through my teeth, but my body feels electric. "That's quite . . . Official."

"It is, isn't it?"

"I hate to remind you, but we haven't even really been on a date."

"Are you sure?" he asks, and I can hear the smile in his voice. "I think we've had two, maybe three."

"Oh yeah? Which ones are you counting?"

"Magnolia, will you come to Thanksgiving?"

"Am I your girlfriend?"

"Yes."

"Then, I will. But first, you have to take me on a date."

I return downstairs, giddy, with fire coursing through my veins. I feel ignited, something I haven't been accustomed to in a long time. It's the joy of having a person you can confide in after you've lost your best friend. It's the realization that you're not trying to replace who you lost, you're just trying to feel again. It's Theo.

I slip back into my chair and am met with anticipated

stares. Dad brings a string of spaghetti to his mouth but drops it before he eats it in favour of studying me. His lips quirk upward slowly, and I look down at my plate to hide the grin on my own face.

"I like seeing you like this," Dad says. "Don't you think she's just positively hyperchromic, Goldie?"

Mom blinks at Dad like she often does when he uses floral terms. "If that means she's glowing, then yes."

"Intense colour, yes."

I laugh and let myself bask in the feeling. "Do you want to meet my boyfriend, Dad?"

On October 3, we finally have our date. I struggle to find an outfit and wind up relying on Poppy's tastes to pick something. I lay two shirts and two dresses on the floor for her to choose from. I should have expected she'd go for the one adorned in sequins.

As I lift it over my head, I realize it's the dress I bought for the Holiday Showcase I never went to two years ago. A piece of my heart breaks, at the same time as I gain the certainty that Iris must have wanted me to wear this tonight as my chance to start over. It's emerald-green with long ballooned sleeves, and hits at mid-thigh. I look like a green disco ball, and I can't say I mind.

Am I overdressed? Yeah, probably. But with my hair flowing in waves down my back and my body glittering like a thousand stars, it doesn't matter. We're going out and I feel good.

The doorbell rings at exactly six o'clock. I can almost picture Theo standing on the doorstep, waiting until exactly the right time. I slip into a cheap pair of black wedge heels and make my way downstairs. My dad has opened the door already, Poppy balanced on his hip.

"Apple Friend!" Poppy shrieks. She reaches out to hug Theo, nearly throwing my dad off balance.

I rush down the stairs, surprisingly not toppling down them in my heels, and steady Dad from behind. He smiles at me graciously, then turns back to Theo, who has relinquished a delighted Poppy from her hug.

"So you're the apple friend," Dad says.

My cheeks flush and I hide my embarrassed smile behind my hand. Theo takes it in stride, laughing because it's the first time he's heard Poppy's nickname for him.

"That's me. But I prefer to go by Theo." He extends a hand to my dad, and they shake.

Mom appears at Dad's side, shocking me. I have no idea where she came from, especially so silently when her default around the house is unintentionally loud thumps. Her eyes light up in recognition upon seeing Theo. She's never seen us together, but seeing as she teaches his daughter, she must know of him, and by the look on her face, she must know good things.

"Mrs. Callas," Theo says, extending the same hand.

My mom wraps her arms around him, instead. I gasp and hold my hand out as if I'll stop her, fully knowing there's nothing I can do about my mom's embarrassing overbearing nature. Theo waves me off and hugs her back.

"Please," Mom says. "You know me. You can call me Goldie."

"All right," he says. "Good to see you again, Goldie."

Dad glances at me to fill in gaps and I whisper to him, "Mom teaches Theo's daughter."

"Daughter?" Dad says, because subtly is not an art he possesses.

Theo's eyebrows rise and he rubs a hand along the back of his neck. "Uh, yeah. I have a daughter. Emma. She's in Mrs.—Goldie's class this year."

"Wow. You must have had her young."

"Dad!" I hiss at the same time Theo says, "I did."

For all my dad's blurt-whatever-comes-to-mind moments, Theo takes it in stride. He's not ashamed of his past because it brought him Emma. The thought makes the butterflies jump in my stomach more so than they already have been.

"Should we get moving?" I ask him, eyes wide, attempting to avoid the parental interrogation that no doubt comes next.

"Yeah!" Theo says and takes a few steps back. He nearly trips over the first step, flailing his arms wildly at the last second, and righting himself with an awkward smile. "We have a reservation to get to."

"Fancy!" Mom says and I can tell she means it from the airy tone of her voice and way she looks at Dad appreciatively. "Take a coat."

I turn to grab a coat from the hall and in that moment Theo disappears. He jogs down the driveway to his car and opens the back door. I fold a tan dress coat over my arm, then return to the door to watch Theo. He reaches into the backseat for something. Mom finds my hand and squeezes it as he rights himself and walks back toward us, two bouquets in hand. His cheeks flush, and I think about how much I fucking adore shy Theo. He deftly climbs our front steps, as if proving he's not going to trip on them again.

When he reaches the top, he hands me a bouquet of calla lilies and my mom a bouquet of wildflowers. Then, he pulls a yellow gerbera daisy from his back pocket and hands it to Poppy. The only difference is that Poppy's flower is fake, and I am eternally grateful for his dad brain the moment she sticks it into her mouth.

Theo smiles. "Forgot them in the car," he says with a laugh. "But I knew they were your favourites, so . . ."

Dad appraises Theo. Flowers are his love language, and to intentionally go out and get someone their favourite flowers gives Theo all the bonus points in my dad's books. And mine. I pass the flowers off to my mom, who whispers the word *keeper* in my ear.

"Thank you," I say, brushing a strand of hair out of my face. I wave to my family. Poppy waves her daisy back at us. "Be back later!"

"Or not," Theo whispers once we're out of earshot.

Chapter Nineteen

Theo takes me to an upscale karaoke bar. Which honestly sounds like a bit of an oxymoron, but apparently their whole gimmick is that you can only go up and sing if you prove you can do it well. You have to sing for an official-looking staff member before they allow you up. It's nothing like karaoke night at the bar. I'm so used to hearing terrible drunken voices every Tuesday night that this is a treat. It's odd, and niche, but it works somehow. It's like being at an unexpected live show.

The only thing that makes it better are the fairy lights and fake leaves that decorate every inch of the restaurant, as if they got their inspiration from the Winter Garden Theatre in Toronto. And the way Theo looks at me . . . His gaze makes me feel as though I'm the only person he wants to sit next to for the rest of his life, even on a first date, even when he's nervous, even through whatever the hell life throws at us.

"So how does your dad feel about me?" Theo asks, just after our dinners arrive. Shrimp scampi for him (because fish are acceptable now that Emma has migrated to pescatarianism) and prime rib with a gorgeous golden baked potato for me.

I pause just before my fork stabs my potato. Theo's eyes are inquisitive, with just a hint of anxiety clouding them.

"Why? Did you think he didn't like you?" I ask.

He shrugs. "I wasn't sure. He seemed surprised by Emma."

I suck in a breath and bite my lip. Theo brings a piece of shrimp to his mouth. There's no way in hell my dad will dislike Theo, especially after the flowers, but I get the nerves swirling in the pit of Theo's stomach. The same jumble in mine at the thought of meeting his whole family next weekend.

"Theo, you brought everyone flowers. The man loves you. But, yeah, he was surprised. That's probably my bad. I didn't tell them much about you, and Mom only knew because she teaches Emma." I squeeze my eyes shut and groan as I realize what I've said. "I get stupid protective of my own peace when I first start going out with someone. My parents love to interrogate my boyfriends, and I shouldn't worry because they've never driven anyone away before . . . But, I don't know, I'm always a little worried at first. I didn't want that to happen with you."

When I look up again, Theo is trying to hide a smirk. He unsuccessfully disguises a laugh as a cough.

"You're cute," he says.

"You're the one who was being cute first," I joke.

Fears abated, we tuck into our food. Unlike Joey from *Friend*s, we share from each others' plates. A shrimp for me, a creamy bit of potato for him. The food is exquisite. Cooked to perfection, bursting with flavour, and my favourite: appropriately buttery and fluffy on the baked potato front. We agree halfway through devouring our plates that their chocolate torte would be the only suitable dessert choice.

"You look like you belong here," Theo says, breaking the post-dinner, pre-dessert silence. I'd been enthralled by the ivy draping a column by the entrance, the shimmering lights reflecting on the grand piano, the thrum of the live music playing, waiting for someone to take the stage. "I've never seen anyone's eyes shine like that. I'm so glad I brought you here. You're beautiful."

My cheeks go red under his intense gaze. I take a sip of white wine. "You know, in grade six, someone told me I needed to lose some weight and fix my hair, and then I'd be pretty."

Theo closes his eyes and groans. "You're kidding"

I shrug. "I was eleven, with frizzy hair like most eleven-year-olds, and was the first girl to get boobs and hips. I've carried weight in my midsection since," I say with a slight blush. "Just how I am. Doesn't matter how you're different—if you're different, someone's gonna pick on that."

"But that's just stupid."

"I would have to agree and cannot say her comments did anything wonderful for my self-esteem back then . . . But hey," I say and raise my glass. "At least I look good in this dress."

Theo laughs at the unexpected comment. To be honest, I don't know where it came from. Maybe the glass of wine is going to my head, though I'm not that much of a lightweight, or maybe I'm just feeling myself. It took me years to be okay with my curves. I'm not a celebrity with an unrealistic tiny waist in comparison to my hips. I have the body to support the way I filled out, but twenty-five years in, I can say I'm miles away from the tween who hated her body.

"I worry about that with Emma. I'm sure you've seen her eyes."

"I love her eyes."

"So do I," he says with a far-off grin. "But like you said, they're different, and people don't like that. A boy last year asked what was wrong with her face, and she had no idea what he meant. I don't ever want someone making her feel inferior for something she can't even help."

I reach across the table and find his hand. He lets me hold it easily, entwining our fingers together and placing his other hand overtop.

"She's lucky she has you. I can't imagine someone living with you being insecure. You're so good at making sure everyone's all right."

He sighs and I can see the burden of parenthood on him. "I hope so. She's had some issues since she fell. Literally doesn't want to get back on the horse, and I hate that for her since she loves the animals. I hope I can help her get that confidence back."

"I think you could," I say and take a deep breath. "If I'm being honest, I think you've done a bit of that for me." He brings my hand to his lips and kisses it, sending shivers through my body. I gaze longingly at the stage. "I might be about to do something stupid."

He drops my hand as I stand and cocks his head to the side.

I'm going to sing.

Elation fills my body the second I step off the stage. Pure, unadulterated joy. Theo's face lights up like I've never seen it. In the polite applause after my song, Theo is standing, clapping, and cheering as loudly as he can. I run to him. Jump into his arms. Kiss him with every ounce of passion I feel.

"Come on," he says into my mouth. "Let's go home."

Dessert be damned.

We keep contact with each other on the way to his house. His hand stays firmly planted on my thigh, just under the hem of my dress. I absently wonder if he can feel the heat coming off me, which only makes me burn more. At the stoplight a few streets before his house, I unbuckle my seatbelt, pull his face towards mine, and mould my mouth to his. He groans and pulls away only because someone honks behind him.

I laugh, throwing my head back in glee. I don't know what's coursing through me, but I never want it to end. He speeds home and we both stumble out of the car in a daze once it's parked in his driveway.

He pushes me up against his front door and kisses me. I loop my hands around his neck, then tangle them in his hair. His gorgeous, soft, auburn hair. I could play with this hair for days. I could play with him for days, and evidently he feels the same way. I feel him hard against me, and I want nothing more than to rip every inch of clothing off his body. It's as if that thought enters his mind at exactly the same moment, because he pulls back and opens the door, allowing us to let our fantasies become reality. He closes the door then turns to me, eyes roaming over my body, absolutely ravenous.

"Where's Rocket?" I whisper, breathless.

"At my parents' house with Emma. Sleepover."

"So many sleepovers," I say and smirk deviously. I sway my hips as I saunter over to him. His strong arms wrap around my waist. "Is that what we're doing?"

In response, his lips crash onto mine and I let out a hasty moan. My cheeks colour, but he doesn't seem to mind.

We move to the place closest to us, too overcome with desire and adrenaline and whatever else is coursing through our veins: the stairs. He pulls me down on top of him and I gasp. I briefly think about rug burn on my knees, but the thought dissipates almost immediately with his lips on mine, with my body on his, my dress ridden up so far that the only thing separating me from him are his pants and my underwear.

His hands find the zipper at the back of my dress and swiftly unzip it. Cold air hits my bare skin and I shudder. Theo grins and runs his hands along my spine, goosebumps forming in his wake. His fingers return to my upper back and undo my strapless bra. I reach back, pull it off, and discard it on the floor of his front foyer. He pulls my dress off my shoulders and stares at my naked breasts as my nipples go pert in the cool air.

"You have entirely too many clothes on," I tell him and reach for the buttons on his shirt.

I run my hands over the planes of his chest, noting the catch in his breath as I edge closer and closer to the belt of his pants. I bite my bottom lip to hold back a grin and he cups my face, brings me back down to him. I push his shirt off his shoulders as he pulls the lip I was biting between his own teeth. My hands work as busily as his lips do. I undo his belt as he kisses along my jawline. I fumble with the button on his pants as his kisses trail my collarbone, then dip lower to a breast. I tip my head back as his teeth graze my nipple.

"Theo," I breathe and place a hand on his chest. He stops and gazes up at me with such unguarded eyes that I almost forget my train of thought. "I haven't had sex in two years."

He chuckles, then looks down at the ground. "I haven't had sex in seven."

"You're joking."

"I am very much not," he says and meets my eyes so I can see just how serious he is. "There was Emma, and then I just didn't want to have any more accidents. Not that it's a bad thing I got her, but I didn't want to have another kid when the possibility of them not having a mother is very real. I'm not one to have flings, and the past seven years have been figuring out how to be a dad. Relationships weren't a thing for me. And I know all of that can be hard to understand in a relationship and . . . Well, I'm done waiting. I want you too much to wait, and I promise we'll be careful and, man, I can't even think I just want you so bad. I want to—"

I kiss him. "Shut up," I say. "Do you have a condom? I mean, I'm on the pill and if you haven't had a partner in that long then it's just us, but if you want to be extra careful . . ." I laugh. "And now I'm rambling."

"Come upstairs with me," he says.

I don't hesitate.

Chapter Twenty

Light streams through the open curtains in Theo's room. My hair fans out over his pillows, shining golden in the sunlight, while the same light picks out the red in his hair. I study his face, relaxed in the last throes of sleep. His eyelids flutter, probably aware on some level that I'm watching him. I remember how his eyes shut as he climaxed and when they opened again to meet mine, his pupils were dilated, euphoric, and it sent me over the edge. Now, his eyes open sleepily, and a slow smile spreads across his lips.

He reaches out, cups a hand below my jaw, and runs his thumb along my bottom lip. "Good morning."

"Morning," I say and remember this exact scenario from a few days ago, but this time we're naked under his sheets. I draw shapes on the exposed flesh of his chest above the edge of the blanket. "Do you have anywhere to be?"

"I'm free today."

I bite back a smile and prop myself up to see the clock on the bedside table behind him. "I've got an hour."

"That's not nearly enough time for all I want to do to

you, but I guess if that's all we have . . ."

I cover his body with my own, climbing on top of him and fluffing my hair out behind me. I lean down to kiss him, softly, slowly. Agonizingly slow. His hands draw themselves down the bare skin of my back and settle on my hips. I pull back and observe him below my lashes. His eyes are reverent, and with a shockwave of desire that rips through me, I realize I feel as though I'm being worshipped. I mean, if worship was measured by how quickly you can make a guy get an erection.

"You look like an angel in this light," he says. I tip my head toward the window, basking in the first morning rays of light. "All you need is a wind machine and it'd be perfect."

I laugh. "I'm still an angel after last night?"

"You're more of an angel after last night. Felt like I went to heaven."

I still manage to flush, even though this man has seen every single part of me laid bare and made my world shake with the use of his tongue, his fingers . . . Him. I run my hand down his chest, delighting in the moment he shudders when my fingers dip below his navel.

I smirk. "Sex angel. Got it."

"My angel. The way you sang last night . . . That's how I imagine an angel singing." My cheeks heat and I look down. Theo brings a hand up to my chin and makes me look at him. "Why don't you sing anymore?"

It feels as though my stomach drops out from under me as he asks the question. I have two options: answer and ruin the mood, or don't answer and still ruin the mood. I can't blame him for asking. He thought he was complimenting me. I still haven't told him, or anyone for that matter, that my singing is so inherently connected to Iris that it's almost impossible for me to do now. Last night was the first time since she died.

I slide off him and fall onto the bed. Theo props himself up on his side, his hand beneath his chin. His other hand reaches out to me, trailing light touches up my arm, until he finds the back of my head and tangles his fingers there.

"It's complicated," I finally whisper.

"Okay." He nods. He doesn't say anything more, just pulls my body to him and holds me until I have to leave.

As Poppy has lunch, I dial the number I've been avoiding for two years. I eye her from my spot, leaning against the fridge. She crushes noodles of Kraft Dinner beneath her fork, giggling as they slide away. I breathe evenly. In through my nose, out through my mouth. The dial tone rings in my ear, and I wait. This is the third time I've tried to call. The first time I've gotten this far.

"Royal Conservatory of Music at The Glenn Gould School, Rosemary speaking. What can I help you with today?"

I take a deep breath, willing myself not to hang up. "Hi, I was wondering if I could speak to someone at the Office of Registrar. I tried to find their number or email in my records, but all I could find was the general Glenn Gould School number."

"Oh, sure, I could transfer you there if you want. Can I ask what it's about, though, just so I can give them a heads-up? Make sure someone's there who can answer your question."

I pause. I hadn't expected her question. I had only

expected her to give me another number, which I would then call on my own time after having, like, a day to prepare what I was going to say.

"I, uh, I was in the Voice Program two years ago. It was my last year and some things happened where I had to withdraw, well, kind of. I haven't been back since."

In the background, I hear her typing pause. "Uh-huh, okay, so what would you like to chat about today?"

"I want to know the process of reenrolling."

"When you withdrew, did you talk to the Head of the Vocal Department?"

I sigh. "No, I didn't."

"All right, then the Office of Registrar won't be able to help you, unfortunately. You'll have to speak to the Head of the Vocal Department to reenrol."

"What? Why?"

"Ultimately, she's in charge of who stays and goes at that stage of the program. If you were in your last year, I'm sure you know how small and close-knit the group is. Arielle takes pride in how she operates the program, so all decisions are hers." Dead air crackles over the phone as neither of us speaks. "I can give you her number or email. She doesn't do phone meetings, so you'll have to set something up."

I shake my head, even though she can't see it. "No, that's all right. I already have her number, thanks."

"Sorry I couldn't be of more help. I hope you find what you need when you speak to Arielle."

I hang up the phone and stare down at it in my hand. I'm half tempted to throw it across the room, but that would only make Poppy do the exact same thing with her food. So, instead, I slam it down in its base beside the toaster. I wipe away the tears that come so Poppy doesn't see. I'm not sure if they're from sadness or frustration or something in between.

As much as I loved that program . . .

As much as I loved my life then . . .

As much as I loved Arielle . . .

There is no way she's going to let me back into the program after I walked away without a word.

Chapter Twenty-One

I throw on a sweater dress, because I intend to eat a lot, and jazz it up with a scarf. I'm on weirdly unsteady ground. I've never been in a relationship where I've felt this good and secure this early on. I probably would have said no to a Thanksgiving dinner if it were anyone else, but this is Theo. And he is the best. But after that call a few days ago, I am decidedly not feeling my best.

And yes, the thought of meeting someone's entire family for the first time at Thanksgiving dinner—the dinner of top tension—is incredibly daunting.

"You're not taking Poppy, right?" Mom asks when I finally make my way downstairs and into the kitchen. She's peeling potatoes for our dinner tomorrow.

I guess another bonus of being invited to Thanksgiving is two dinners. Double the food.

"No, it's just me."

Mom turns to me and smiles. She dries her hands off on a towel, then begins fixing me. She fluffs out my hair and straightens my scarf. She steps back and assesses.

"What're you doing for shoes?"

I glance down at my feet and wiggle my sock-clad toes. "Uh, I was thinking a low boot. Doesn't matter. I put on the knee socks since we're inside anyway."

"Then you're good. You look perfect." I smile at the compliment and turn on my heel to leave. "Don't forget the cookies!"

Mom didn't want me to show up empty handed, so she baked her special cinnamon chocolate chip cookies last night. Honestly, I think it was just an excuse to get something out of the way for our dinner, but I appreciate the vote of confidence in my love life. My plan was just to take a bottle of wine—the customary house gift. Now I have both.

As I open the door to leave, having said goodbye to all members of my family, Poppy comes running. When I realize what she's holding, I laugh. She stops in front of me and holds out an apple she apparently stole from the fresh bag my mom picked to make an apple pie. Her turned-up chin, pursed lips, and scrunched-up nose show that she's undeniably proud of herself.

"Is this for our apple friend, Pops?" I ask and she nods enthusiastically. "Thank you! I'm sure he'll love it!"

"Bye bye!" Poppy says and closes the door on me.

I stare at the closed door for a moment, then laugh. Poppy is an odd little creature, but I'm so glad I get to know her. I skip down the stairs toward the Bug and set the plate of cookies, bottle of wine, and apple on the roof of my car while I dig within the depths of my purse for my keys. I curse the creator of this dress for not including pockets. After a good minute, I open the door and shove everything into the backseat. I grab my phone before sliding into the driver's seat.

I pull up Theo's sister's address on my phone. If Thanksgiving were at his house, I'd probably just walk, but as it stands I have a hopefully fifteen-minute drive ahead of me. Though considering the residential traffic and construction between Oakville and Milton, it may very well be longer.

I drive along the suburban streets until I hit farmland, a sure sign that Milton is on the horizon. It's an odd sort of town, flanked by stretches of vacant farmland on either end. Twenty years ago, the town was ridiculously small, more farm than city. But now people have flocked here, trampling down trees and flat land to put up houses. Theo's sister, Rachael, and her husband, Ethan, moved into one of these new developments last year. I understand the need for more affordable housing, trust me, I do. But as I drive through roads lined with trees changing from green to shades of red, yellow, and orange, I can't help but feel a little disheartened.

Eventually I emerge from the trees and come across the townhouse development I'm pretty sure is the one I'm looking for. I pause at a stoplight and pick up my phone to look at the address again. I'm probably about a minute away now. I just have to find the right street. Which leads me to the discovery that their street has no parking left, certainly due to the holiday, so I drive past their house and wind up two streets over.

When I finally show up at the doorstep of the stacked townhouse, I'm sweaty. This October, much like the past three Octobers, has been warm. While festive, my sweater dress, scarf, and boot combo is a bit too hot for the weather. I wrestle with the wine and cookies as I find the doorbell. There's sweat on my forehead, but I can't wipe it away because my hands are full and everything I'm holding is breakable. Why my mom needed to send the cookies along on her fancy glass harvest plate, I do not know.

A woman with long red hair, brilliantly blue eyes, and a baby on her hip answers the door. Though I can't remember ever seeing her before, I know this must be Theo's older sister Rachael.

"Hello! You're Magnolia, right?" Rachael asks and opens the door farther at my nod. "Here, let me take something!"

"You have your hands full, too. I promise I'm fine with these. Though, they are for you. The wine and cookies."

"That's so nice of you! I'll definitely have some of that wine later. It's been a long while since I've had a nice glass of, what is that, Riesling?"

I laugh as I slide out of my boots. "You know your wine."

"I would hope so! I worked at Trius for three summers during university."

"Well, this is from Peller, so you're pretty damn accurate."

Rachael pantomimes a cheer as her baby chews on his hands. She notices me watching him and colour comes to her cheeks. "Sorry, I got ahead of myself. I think you may have assumed I'm Rachael, but if not, hi, I'm Rachael." She extends a hand but makes an awkward wave when she realizes I can't shake at the moment. "And this is my little goober, Parker."

Parker pulls his hands out of his mouth with a long and glorious stream of saliva. Goober is right. I smile and crouch to his level. I introduce myself to him and pull a funny face, successfully making him laugh. I officially have two more people on my side should I need them.

We walk into the kitchen and the noise level significantly

rises. I place the wine and cookies down next to the sink where Rachael gestures. From my vantage point, I can see over the kitchen island and into the dining and family rooms. Theo has three siblings, two of which are married with kids, and the last one, as Theo estimates, is on the verge of an engagement. It seems I'm the last to arrive. I can only guess who is who, predominantly relying on the fact that all the Hennessy siblings appear to have varying shades of red hair. I spot Emma playing Hungry Hungry Hippos with two boys who look about a year or two younger than she is. Theo bends down from his position in the chair behind her and whispers something in her ear that makes her switch arms on the hippo's back. When he looks up again, he spots me and breaks into a grin. I easily return it.

As Theo gets up, his brothers take note, zero in on me, and start whistling.

"It's Theo's girlfriend!!" one of them calls. "Guys, it's Theo's girlfriend!"

"Everyone! Everyone! Look who finally took the bachelor off the market!" the other yells.

They both continue to rib him as he comes into the kitchen. I dissolve into a fit of giggles as they make fun of him. I can see the hesitation in Theo's body language as he plants himself in front of me, wondering if his brothers are too much. But I adore it. Sibling banter is the best and, of course, as the youngest he would get the worst of it.

Theo's arm wraps around my waist as he leans in to kiss me. But I catch the finger he shoots his brothers before I close my eyes. I laugh into the kiss.

"Happy Thanksgiving!" I say and hold out Poppy's shiny red apple. "This is from your apple friend."

Theo bites into the apple with exaggerated fervour. "Tell her thank you from me. Also, this is really good!"

"It's fresh! My mom picked it yesterday. So, do I get introductions?"

Theo turns and keeps his hand firmly placed on my lower back as he walks me into the thick of it. He points out Ethan, the chef, who is bustling around the kitchen, relinquishing zero control of the dinner to anyone other than himself. Already sitting at the table, enjoying their cooking reprieve, are Theo's parents.

"These are my parents, Ruth and Joshua." Theo says.

I can see him in both of them. He gets the red hair from his mom, though his dad also has some auburn strands in his slightly greying, otherwise dark-brown hair. The beard is all his dad and, I note, is the way all the Hennessy boys seem to do it. The icy eyes that both Rachael and Theo have also come from their dad. Both parents are lanky, with long legs stretched out underneath the table.

"It's so nice to finally meet you," Ruth says and stands to envelope me in a hug.

"Oh," I say and wrap my arms around her as well. I eye Theo next to me with a smirk. "I take it that means Theo's said some things about me."

"Theo gushes like a little girl," one of his brothers calls from the other side of the room.

"Shut up, Ian!" Theo quips.

I place my hand on Theo's chest. "No, it's cute. I like it."

He visibly relaxes at my touch, and I bite my bottom lip to keep myself from grinning. I turn back to his parents and shake hands with his dad, who also seems excited to meet me.

"Theo tells us you're a singer," Joshua says.

I blush. "Maybe someday."

Ruth's eyes light up and she reaches out to me once more. "Magnolia, dear, we're not a house of maybes. You're already a singer. You sing. You're a singer."

My cheeks turn bright-red as my heart soars. Theo's grip on my waist tightens slightly and I smile up at him. He guides me into the bustling family room where the rest of the introductions come swiftly, with a heavy dose of teasing from his brothers. There's Ian, who threatens to bring out old embarrassing photo albums, his wife Christina, and their twin five-year-olds Hunter and Hayden. Then comes Gabe, who offers to tell the story of how Theo shit his pants at an amusement park when he was twenty, and his boyfriend Jude. I laugh at each anecdote, Theo clinging to my side, going more and more red in the face. Me, I seem to fall harder with each conversation and apparently get initiated into the family when both Ian and Gabe point out how dreamy I look.

"Magnolia!" Emma calls as I settle in the same chair that Theo vacated. "Would you sit next to me at dinner? I want to show you all the signatures on my cast."

I readily agree. Theo and I were the first to sign her cast the night she got it. Below my signature and flower, Theo added his name with a heart. Emma holds out her arm, then stands. She slips her good hand into mine and leads me to my new official spot at the table.

Chapter Twenty-Two

"Honestly, what is it about men that makes them so stupid?" Rachael asks, sitting down next to me on the front porch.

During dinner, Rachael mentioned the frogs that live in the pond across the street from their house, which led to Ian musing on how high and far he could jump, which led to Gabe suggesting they test that out. All the Hennessy men, plus Ethan and Jude, stand in the middle of the street, ironing out the rules of their bet. Theo points to the garage, then the end of the driveway.

"There's something in their DNA that just makes them that way," Ruth says to her daughter, then pauses. She laughs from her spot on the bench next to the front door. "Or rather, there's something lacking. They're missing the gene that tells them not to do things."

I smirk. The boys grin at each other like they've solved the mysteries of the universe, if the mysteries were how far a person could jump. They hold out their hands and shake, clearly having decided on the numeric value of this ridiculous task.

"Did anyone do this as a sport when they were younger?"

I ask. "Like, long jump, I mean."

Rachael snorts, which makes Parker giggle on her lap. She bounces her knee. "No, we were very firmly a hockey family here. It's a wonder I never dated a hockey guy, eh Mom?"

Ruth rolls her eyes and Rachael bites back a smile. "Don't even get me started on who you dated, young lady."

"You don't have to worry about them now. Just focus on your other children giving you heart attacks. I'm past being stupid, but luckily for you and your band of boys, they'll never grow out of it."

I can't hold back the snicker. That's something so very *eldest child* to say. Ruth reaches out and clips her daughter on the head jokingly. They both laugh. Rachael stares at her mother as if this is the most obvious thing in the world, and quite frankly it probably is. Raising boys seems a helluva lot more stressful than girls. Because let's be real, the stressful thing about girls is when they bring boys into the mix.

"So what you're saying is you have no idea who'll win," I say.

"I think Gabe has a shot," Christina pipes up. She sits a stair lower than me and Rachael, staring at her phone as if this is something her boys do regularly. "If only because it was his idea. I'm just hoping H&H don't break anything."

"My money's on Jude," Rachael states automatically. "He just seems scrappy and he's not one of my brothers."

"What about your husband?" Ruth asks.

"What about yours?"

"My husband is about to break a hip."

Rachael cackles while Christina cringes. Emma jumps up from her spot next to Ruth and leans against the railing. She tracks the boys as they break from their huddle and meander up to the garage, then sticks her tongue out at Hunter and Hayden.

"I think my dad could win. He has to run for work, so he can at least do the first part right," Emma says, looking back at us.

A slow smile spreads across my face and Ruth catches me. She nods and I draw my gaze toward the step beneath my feet. It's not a bad guess, though.

"All right, ladies," Gabe announces to varying degrees of groans from the four of us and a very attentive Emma. She had no interest in participating, but judging she could do. "Each of us are going to run the length of the driveway, then once we hit the curb, we jump. Whoever jumps the furthest will win one hundred dollars."

The boys cheer and I absently wonder where they got the money, but I don't dwell on it long because I'm sure they scrounged some up from their enviously big pockets. Gabe holds a stick of chalk out to the group. We stare at it impassively.

"Are we supposed to get up?" I ask.

The Hennessy women chuckle and Ian claps Theo on the shoulder. Though I hadn't meant to say it out loud, I'm glad we're all thinking it.

"Well, one of you, yes," Gabe says. He brandishes the chalk some more. "You're impartial and we need our jumps marked off."

"Who said we're impartial?" Rachael asks. She raises a perfectly manicured eyebrow at her brother in challenge.

"I'll pick my husband, Christina will pick you, Mom will pick Dad, and Theo actually fairs the best with his two sideline supporters. The only clear loser here is Ian."

"What about Jude?" Gabe asks.

"Jude's the only one I think could actually win."

Jude pumps the air while Ethan cries out against his wife's chosen allegiance. My cheeks hurt from the laughter I've let out over the past few hours.

"Hey, Em!" Theo calls. Emma snaps her attention from Gabe to her dad. "Would you mind being the official measurer?"

Emma nods enthusiastically and climbs over our clearly not very well-done block of the stairs. She squeezes past me and Rachael, then brushes by Christina, and runs to Gabe. She plucks the chalk deftly from his hands and rests her casted arm on her hip.

"Game on," she says and from her levelled stare at the lined up Hennessys, you can tell she means it. She rushes down to the end of the driveway and raises her arms.

"Anyone have a flag?" Ruth asks.

Rachael shifts from her perch and stares at her front door. "Ethan has a stupid Leafs flag inside. Anyone want to make the effort of getting it?"

Ruth reluctantly gets up from the bench and slinks inside. The boys wait for her return, discussing the order of who runs first and the benefits of Emma choosing vs. age order. Eventually, Theo pulls out his phone and finds a website called Wheel of Names to randomly pick their order.

When Ruth returns two minutes later, the order is set.

Emma runs up to the stairs to meet her and takes the flag that's about the size of her face, emblazoned with a blue maple leaf. She drops the piece of chalk into the front pocket of her windbreaker, then jogs down the driveway once more.

"Emma, you're also our lookout for cars, okay?" her grandpa calls down to her. She shoots him a thumbs-up, then raises her flag.

Each man fails.

None of them make it to their goal of fully crossing the street in one jump, but man, is it fun to watch them try. In spectacularly tragic fashion, Theo successfully runs at full speed down the driveway, but hilariously trips on the edge, falling flat on his face. Emma walks up to him and marks off where the tips of his fingers landed.

He groans as he pushes himself off the ground, brushing his scuffed hands on his jeans. His brothers laugh from afar.

"Was anyone filming that?" Ian yells. "I would pay good money to see that over and over again."

"We could make Theo go viral with that. Holy shit," Gabe says through roaring laughter.

Theo lopes back up to the house and settles down in the spot beside Christina. His cheeks blaze, but he's laughing at himself as hard as the others.

"Come here, ya big loser," I say and pull his face toward mine for a quick kiss. He pulls back and I grin then whisper, "I got that on camera."

Chapter Twenty-Three

"I hope you know I'm living vicariously through this relationship," Hanna tells me as we walk around the grounds of the Milton Fall Fair with Poppy.

"You know you're in a relationship, right?" I ask.

Hanna laughs, which makes Poppy, who clings to her arms, giggle as well. "Oh, I know." She flashes me the princess cut diamond on her left hand. "But you're at that cute stage of a relationship. The honeymoon phase where everything is glorious and fun and hot."

"It was only hot that one time. I haven't seen him in, like, six days," I say.

"I dunno," she says, eyes boring into mine. "I think you guys sound pretty hot, sex or not. Like, you're absolutely eye fucking each other." I widen my eyes and nod toward Poppy. "Oh, sorry, uh, eye screwing. I mean, you're in that stage where you look at each other and are mentally screwing. Am I right?"

"I would do more than mentally screw him if I could."

"Tell me why you're with me tonight and not him

again?"

"Because he's a dad and he promised to go out with Emma," I say as if this should be obvious to her.

It's one of the things I like most about Theo. He's such a great, attentive father. I'm lucky to share him with Emma. Hanna appreciates this too. There's nothing she likes better than a good dad, especially when working so closely with pregnancies and babies.

Poppy tugs on Hanna's hair and she flinches away. I open my mouth to tell Poppy to be gentle, but her little voice rings out before mine.

"Anna, look!" Poppy says, not quite having mastered the *H* sound. She points to a line for the Pluck A Duck game. "Apple Friend!"

I can't help the laugh that bubbles out of me. I hope she never calls him anything other than "Apple Friend." Hanna scans the crowd but can't identify where to look with his back turned away. I recognize yet another plaid shirt, the broad back, red hair, and of course, Emma standing next to him with her arm casted in purple. Poppy squirms out of Hanna's arms and makes a mad dash to where Theo stands about ten feet away.

"I hope you know she's replaced you as the favourite," I say to Hanna before running after Poppy.

Poppy pulls on Theo's shirt until he turns, ironically holding a candy apple. I appear next to Poppy and lift her up so she can truly express her glee. She zeroes in on his new apple and makes a delighted shriek.

"Poppy wanted to say hi to her apple friend," I say with a smirk.

Theo grins warmly at us and holds out the glossy apple on a stick. "Guilty as charged."

From the corner of my eye, I notice Hanna and Emma chatting quietly. Though, with the noise of the fair around us—announcers at games, chatter from fair goers, screams from those on rides, bleats of various farm animals—they'd have to speak pretty loudly for us to hear. The way they lean into each other and smirk conspiratorially makes me certain they're exchanging more than just pleasantries. Theo catches my gaze and spins to face his daughter and my best friend plotting together.

"Uh . . . Yes?" he says, head cocked to one side.

Emma blushes as Hanna straightens with zero shame. They both smile innocently at Theo. I shift my weight to my other hip, better balancing Poppy, and wait for them to reveal yet another *Parent Trap* plan.

"I want to go on the Ferris wheel!" Emma announces. "With Poppy."

My eyes shoot to Hanna. She wiggles her eyebrows at me, and I laugh behind my hand.

"You've never been on a Ferris wheel," Theo says with obvious suspicion lacing his voice.

"That's why I want to go on it! You and Magnolia should go too."

Theo turns and looks at the ride. The rainbow carriages swing in the early evening wind. Lights snap on around us, illuminating the rides and games in glorious fanfare. He swallows. I place a hand on his chest. He meets my eyes and gives me a small smile before turning back to his daughter.

"If you really want to, then sure. But you have to stay with me or Mags."

"I can take them." Hanna volunteers and steps forward to take Poppy from me. "You're welcome," she whispers in my ear.

The three of them head off to the Ferris wheel without our full permission. I admire the quick thinking, and I'm even more flattered that Emma has so readily accepted me for her dad.

"I think you have a little matchmaker on your hands."

"You think?" Theo laughs. "She asks about you constantly. Keeps trying to convince me to ship her off to my parents and invite you over. She said she'd make cupcakes for you if you came over."

My eyes light up. "Can I make them with her? I love cupcakes."

"I'm sure she'd like it if you offered."

Theo finds my hand and entwines our fingers. We walk aimlessly toward the Ferris wheel, but I can feel the hesitation in his steps. It's as though his feet get heavier and heavier as we go. I slip the silk scrunchie off my wrist and pull my hair back into a ponytail. Whether or not we make it to the Ferris wheel, I don't want my hair flying around, getting in our way. I stop in front of Theo just before we join the line. Hanna and the girls are nearly at the front.

"You know we don't have to go on it, right?" I ask him. He raises his eyebrows in surprise. "Gabe told me the poop story. I gather you don't like heights. But even if I didn't know, I can tell by how you're acting right now."

"That was not on a Ferris wheel," Theo says with a laugh.

"No, it was on a drop tower, which makes it worse. But it's still a height thing, right?"

His gaze trails slowly up the length of the Ferris wheel, tracking a particularly wobbly blue car. "It is a height thing."

"Are you a bad flier too?"

"Only if I'm at the window. Generally, I can ignore the fact that I'm floating 30,000 feet in the air if I can't see it. But right now, the thought kind of makes me want to vomit."

I scan the rides around us. Most of them are a bit extreme. All things that shoot you up in the air for a thrill, then send you right back down again and again. I spot something potentially friendly behind the Ferris wheel and stand on my tiptoes to see what's beneath the lit-up circus top of the ride.

"Are those teacups?" I ask Theo. He squints. "Do you want to go on the teacups? I promise I won't spin you too hard."

"Spin away," he says.

We run off to the teacups and I shoot Hanna a text. I don't check for a response, especially since we can see her from our ride. There's barely a line for the teacups, so we walk on easily. Theo hurries to a bright orange cup, insisting it's the one that will spin the fastest.

"Okay," he says as the bells go off and the ride begins to move. "You say you won't spin me too fast, but can I spin you?"

I lean back against the plastic bench of the cup and make a show of folding my arms behind my head and resting against them. "I dare you."

Theo grins like an imp and takes hold of the metal wheel between us. I quickly learn that I can't be casual because his spins are anything but casual. I grip onto the sides of the ride and giggle hysterically as the world twirls past us. The butterflies in my stomach feel like they're running a marathon, and I'm pretty sure it's a combo of his joy and the ride's movement. I can't take my eyes off him. Everything is a blur around us except for him. I see Theo in great clarity. I can tell from the way his eyes bore into mine, the way his smile creases the corners of them, the way his laughter keeps bubbling out of him that he's feeling the same way.

And somehow, in this moment, I don't care how early it is. I'm in love with him.

Chapter Twenty-Four

Karaoke night rolls around, and I'm on a weird high combined with a weird low. I've never really known how to describe emotions that feel entirely opposite from each other. How do you tell someone you're feeling gloriously happy but also extremely dissatisfied? Can those two things coexist?

As I wipe down a table next to the bathroom, I know they can.

I hate it here.

It's a realization that came in a snap. It wasn't gradual. It wasn't a series of little things that built up and blew up. It was just a passing thought that lingered. That I realized was true. That I fixated on. And then nearly choked on air when it settled.

"You good?" Chloe asks. She flips the white streak of hair out of her face and tucks it behind an ear. "You've been cleaning the same spot for five minutes."

I stare down at the overly shiny table and huff. I pull my phone from the back pocket of my jeans and peek at the time. Nearly 7:30 p.m. Karaoke starts at exactly eight.

I have time for a miniature breakdown.

"Honestly? No. I'm not good." I pause and let my words sink in, for both me and her. "I don't think I've been good in a while."

"Oh, honey," she says and wraps an arm around my shoulders.

I follow her through the pub, behind the bar, and into the break room. She plops down next to me on the ugly stained and discoloured corduroy couch that's been at UFO since it opened forty years ago. I wrinkle my nose. Most of my time here has been spent avoiding this couch and its ominous stains and stories. But I get over it quickly, life crisis apparently more pressing, and drop my head into my hands.

"What's going on?" Chloe asks.

I sigh and try to collect my thoughts. They come out in a long stream of air. "I'm just not happy."

"Girl, you know you deserve happiness just as much as anyone else. If you're not happy, then leave him."

My brain stutters over her words, vehemently agreeing with the first part and desperately puzzling at the last. I slowly straighten up and turn my face towards her. Her hand, chipped nail polish and all, rests on my knee, while her face creases in worry.

"I'm sorry, what?" I eventually ask.

"There's nothing that says you have to stay in a relationship if you're unhappy. You've been together for, what? Like a month?"

I shrug. "More or less. But I—"

"Then you owe him absolutely nothing."

"It's not about him, though." I find my voice. It comes out stronger than I intend. Defensive and slightly angry. My cheeks colour and I turn to stare at the whiteboard where we write about shitty customers, make jokes, and draw dicks. We're a very professional workplace. "Sometimes I think he's the only person keeping me sane right now. But he's also the one who made me realize I wasn't happy. I just feel so . . . stuck here. My life feels so sedentary. It's like I haven't moved forward at all in two years. My life has just been frozen while everyone else hits their milestones."

Chloe's gaze burns a hole in my head, but I refuse to look at her as she digests my words. "I don't know what to say to that."

"Yeah, same." That breathy laugh comes back to me. I can feel pressure behind my eyes, waiting on tears to fall. But I refuse to have another full-on breakdown at work. This miniature one will have to do. I wipe at my nose.

"Is that the first time you've said that out loud?"

I nod. "I've felt it for a while, but I haven't been able to articulate it. Or I've pushed it down because I felt like I had to. I don't really know which one it is. All I know is that this isn't new. And being happy with Theo made me address how incredibly unhappy I am with everything else."

"Is that good? Like, that you're in a relationship that makes you question everything you've loved previously?"

Her words make me pause again. Not in consideration, but to wonder why she wants to shit on my one source of happiness right now. Maybe she's just not the person to talk to about this. I know she's had her struggles with her parents cutting contact from her after she dropped out of university, but she's happy with her life and that's all that matters. Our versions of happiness completely differ. Chloe has always been happy to work odd jobs, like the pub, for a year so she can travel with everything she's made. I don't just want to travel, though. I want someone to spend my life with, and I want something solid to work towards. I don't know if I want to sing again. I don't know if that was my dream or Iris's. I just know I want something more than this.

"You should come to Asia with me," Chloe says, breaking the silence I created. My head snaps toward her and she grins. "Come on, it'll be so fun! I'm aiming to go in January and take a few months. Maybe four or five. I'm thinking Malaysia, Singapore, Philippines, Taiwan, Vietnam, Cambodia, and Thailand. Maybe Laos, I haven't decided yet. But you should come. It could be like our Euro Trip 2.0."

I lick my lips and try to think of anything to say. I know now that my trip to Europe, as much as it was the one that Iris and I planned all those years ago and I felt duty bound to take in her honour, was really just me running. I couldn't face that she wasn't here, and I'd given up everything I'd ever worked toward in my life in one fell swoop, so I left. I know that if I say yes to Chloe now, I'll be doing the exact same thing all over again.

"Thank you for the offer," I say. "But I don't think travel is in my cards right now. I think I need to figure myself out, finally."

Chloe shrugs and pushes herself off the couch. "I've always found that travelling is a great way to find yourself." She turns to face me, standing between me and the whiteboard so I can no longer stare at it. "Maybe it's being here that bothers you. You were different when I met you. You seemed so much brighter."

"That's because going on that trip connected me to Iris." I brush my fingers against my waterline, trying to wipe away the tears threatening to fall without ruining my makeup. "We never planned an Asia trip, so going there isn't going to light me up like following Iris's European itinerary."

"Why did that work in Europe and not here, then? I'm sure there are things here that remind you of her. I mean, you have Poppy. She's a literal mini of your sister from everything you've told me."

I nod but don't have the energy to tell her why that's different. It hurts to come home from an experience that helped you start to work through your grief, only to find that no one else at home was able to do that. All they were able to do was brush it under the rug and pretend they only ever had one daughter. Even now, with Iris's birthday this week and the second anniversary of her death in two months, no one has said anything. Both my parents are mute about these facts, and it drives me nuts. But if that's how they're choosing to process, then I don't know if I can even say anything. Who am I to dictate how everyone should act?

"Sometimes it hurts to look at Poppy," I say, surprising both of us.

Chloe manages a laugh. "Yeah, kids are like that sometimes."

I take a shaky breath and nod again. I'm not going to explain it to her. I'm not going to explain it to anybody. I stand from the couch, eyeing the clock on the wall behind Chloe.

"It's time for karaoke."

Chapter Twenty-Five

"Can I run something by you?" Theo asks the minute I pick up the phone. "And feel free to say no."

I wrinkle my nose and pause on my way to pick up a bouquet of flowers wrapped in green tissue paper. I should probably know what kind they are after twenty-five years of living with my father, the florist, but I don't. I also probably should have gone to him if I wanted flowers, but I didn't.

"Sure, I guess."

"You don't sound so sure," he says, hesitant.

I laugh, then cup my hand around the phone and whisper into it. "Just makes it sound like you want to try some weird kinky thing."

"I thought we—Never mind, it's not . . . that . . . Are you in public?"

My eyes scan the grocery store. No one's so much as looking at me or even caring that I'm on the phone.

"Yes."

"Okay. Doesn't matter. As I said, this has nothing to do

with anything."

"Are you around Emma?"

"Yes."

"Ah," I say with a giggle, "then I will refrain from mentioning anything kinky."

"Thank you. So anyway, I made the mistake of showing Emma the original Addams Family movie and—"

"Why is that a mistake? It's a classic."

I pick up another bouquet of flowers. Carnations, I think. A peppery sort of scent fills my nostrils. I sneeze almost instantly. Okay, not those. I put them back in their place and meander around the small flower section.

"I'm getting there," Theo says. "Emma wants to be Wednesday for Halloween now."

"Doesn't everyone want to be her? That show made her cool again." I bend to inspect more flowers, but nothing really suits what I'm going for.

"So I was wondering what you were doing for Halloween and, maybe, wanted to know if you wanted to do a group costume."

I straighten. "Oh. Can I be Morticia? I mean, unless you want to be her."

Since I was already out, I volunteered to meet Theo at Value Village. They have a tiny section of costumes, but anyone who's anyone knows you can build a costume from thrifted clothing pieces. I'd also suggested Fabricland, but Theo figured it was easier to get pieces than totally create them from scratch. And he'd be right, especially in the case of the Addams Family.

I walk through the doors of Value Village and scan the aisles for Theo and Emma. I know I'm early, but I was already out and right next door at Metro, so it's only natural I would be here first. I wander through the store, challenging myself to find the wackiest thing someone thrifted. In the span of twenty minutes, I find a piggy bank with the words "Lazy Money" etched onto it, a silver-plated hand statue commemorating someone's engagement, a binder decorated with Joe Jonas circa 2009, a tie-dye shirt with a rose on it that just says "Lust," and a severely discoloured water bottle from the year 2000.

I'm inspecting the rusty stains on the bottle when I see movement at the automatic front doors. Two people walk in, and I'm almost certain they're Theo and Emma. I place the bottle back on its shelf, wiping my hands on my jeans, and head toward the entrance to get a better view. Theo wears a T-shirt with the town's paramedic emblem embroidered on the chest. And as much as I love seeing fabric form around his biceps and as much as I love his arms and hands and everything they can do . . .

"What is wrong with you?" I ask.

Emma smirks and Theo jumps, not having spotted me just yet. "What? What did I do?"

"You're wearing a T-shirt."

He stares at me like he doesn't know what I'm talking about. His eyes trail up my body, from the riding boots, to the forest-green jean jacket, to the same scarf I wore to Thanksgiving, then he looks down at his own outfit. Emma laughs next to him, appropriately dressed for fall.

"I'm wearing jeans as well," he says, not getting it.

"It's, like, eight degrees and you're wearing a T-shirt."

"And jeans!"

I roll my eyes and catch Emma do the same.

"Don't even bother," she says. "He wears shorts in winter."

"All good Canadians do!" Theo jokes, holding his hands up in surrender. "But neither of you are summer babies. You don't know what it's like to run hot."

"I guess I'm just very very cold," I say and wiggle my eyebrows.

Emma interrupts before Theo can protest further. "I already have a black dress," she says and starts walking away. Theo, used to his daughter's pace, easily walks with her. I jog to catch up despite being branded Tall for a Girl. "So I don't need that. I do need something with a collar, though. What do you need?"

"I guess I need a floor-length black dress. And a wig. Poppy needs a striped shirt." My gaze shifts to Theo. He meets my eyes and winks. "You need a suit."

"I have a suit."

"Do you have a pinstripe suit?"

"If I say yes, will you judge me?"

I laugh. Emma starts sifting through racks of dresses, presumably searching for something for me.

"No . . . Unless it's a judge-able reason."

"What's judge-able?"

"Why do you have a pinstripe suit, Theo?"

Theo shrugs. His cheeks go a little pink. "I hosted a 1920s murder mystery party a few years back."

"He made me the murderer," Emma supplies and turns around with a hand on her hip. "I was three."

"You made a very good murderer, my dear," Theo says

in a vaguely British accent.

"You know gangsters aren't British, right?" I ask.

"I do know that." His neck reddens this time. I return his grin. "That's just the only accent I can do."

Emma pulls out a long lacy dress. She passes it over to me. The neck plunges a little too deep for my comfort, but even that is perfect for Morticia. The sleeves balloon at the wrists and flow out, making the lace look like a spider web on both arms. Theo runs his hand along the lace, then looks at me appreciatively.

"You should get that."

"I have to try it on first," I say and sling it over my arm. "I mean, it looks good, but I'm worried about the neck and I think it might be too clingy."

Theo kisses me just below my ear and whispers, "You should get that."

My skin tingles as he walks away to catch up with Emma. I pull a few other black dresses off the racks, none so Morticia-y, but they're long and they'll do the trick. I spot Theo and Emma a few rows over. Theo meets my eyes and holds up a striped Poppy-sized shirt. I shoot him a thumbs-up.

"You need a disembodied hand," I say once I've sidled up next to him.

"A what?"

"You know Thing? The hand that helps Gomez out? You need one."

Emma takes off without warning, crossing the store and showing up in the Halloween section. Theo seems relatively unfazed by her wandering, but I guess you would be after seven years of growing with your child. It's also not as though she's running through the store for the sake of it. She's very focused on the task at hand and, so far, she's found everything we need. Theo walks with me as we join Emma. He finds my free hand at my side and loops his fingers through mine. I squeeze his hand.

"You okay?" Theo asks as we reach the aisle Emma flits through.

I stare at his profile. The sharp lines of his face smoothed out by the softness of his beard. I sigh.

"How do you know there's something wrong with me?" I ask, testing the waters.

"You put on this happy front sometimes, but I can see how tired you are underneath it. Today is one of those days, I think."

I swallow. "When you called . . . I was out picking up flowers for my sister's grave. It's her birthday tomorrow, so I just thought—" I shrug and keep my eyes on Emma, willing myself not to cry. "I haven't been there since her funeral, but it's her birthday and she shouldn't be alone, you know? I don't know."

Theo nods and squeezes my hand again. "I know. If you need company and you're willing to wait until 7:00 or 8:00 p.m., I'll come with you. But I know that's late."

"Thank you," I breathe. "I don't even know if I'll go for sure yet. Maybe I'll just get some irises for my room."

Emma rushes up to us holding the disembodied hand I requested. She passes that to Theo triumphantly then hands me a long black wig, just as victorious. I balance the plastic wig package on top of the dresses and Theo pinches it away with his less full hands. He gives it back to Emma.

"How do you feel about dyeing your hair?"

Chapter Twenty-Six

"Theo, I swear to God, if you ruin my hair I will murder you," I say, sitting on a kitchen chair in his unsurprisingly colourful wallpapered and tiled upstairs bathroom. "I will make your child an orphan. I don't care."

Theo laughs as he shakes one of the bottles in the dye package. I'd agreed to dyeing my hair probably too readily. Theo wasted zero time, bought our thrift store finds, then dragged me and Emma to Shoppers a few box stores down. He stood in the dye aisle completely clueless, pulling out boxes that were too permanent or weren't actually dye. He broke from the group, grabbing something else he needed while Emma and I found the perfect black dye, and, because she wanted to have a little fun, we also grabbed some temporary purple.

"Are you having regrets?" he asks, squeezing my garbage bag-covered shoulders.

I meet his eyes in the mirror. "Maybe. The last time I dyed my hair, it was pink tips in October of 2021. This is much more commitment than pink tips."

Theo squints down at the box. "This says it's temporary."

"Nothing is temporary on blonde hair." I laugh, only half joking. I've had some dye stick for months and alter my colour for years, and that wasn't black. "I'll just have to wash the shit out of it."

"We don't have to do it if you don't want to," he says.

He pauses with the dye bottle in his hand and from my garbage bag vantage point, he looks like a mad scientist. I laugh, maybe a little too enthusiastically, and Theo's eyebrows rise.

"No, I want to," I say when I've regained my composure. I fiddle with a long strand of my hair. I need a haircut. It's been too long, and my hair now sits just past my waist. "I'm sure you can guess why I haven't dyed my hair. Everything comes back to one moment, I guess. But Iris always used to do it for me, back home in our childhood bathroom. I was twelve the first time we dyed our hair together. Ironically, pink streaks. I think the world came out to spite me by making my hair almost the same when she died."

"How'd you guys do it? Did you put on music? Do you want me to get Emma and you guys can dye yours together? The purple just lasts a few days, right?"

My throat closes up at his questions. I furiously blink away tears and swallow down the emotion so I'm able to speak.

"The purple is basically just a spray. It won't last a shower, so it's good intro hair dye." I turn in the chair and tilt my head up toward him. "Thank you, again, for letting me talk about her."

Theo shakes his head as if this is the most nonsensical thing to thank him for. "You don't have to thank me for something that should be second nature. You can talk about her anytime. Or not. Just let me know what you need."

He leans in to kiss me. It's the briefest touch of his lips, but it sets my soul on fire. When he pulls away, I want to pull him down for more, but I know Emma is just a room away and what's on my mind is much more than a simple kiss, so I face the mirror again. I watch him shift to the counter and bend to take one final look at the instructions. He shakes the dye bottle again. I take a deep breath and stare at the fishy border above the mirror that encircles the room.

"You ready?" Theo asks.

An hour later, I resurface from the bathroom with long silky black hair. To Theo's credit, he did a really good job. I'd thought ahead and grabbed two boxes to cover the whole length of my hair. No patches of blonde peek out, just solid raven black. It's been a while since I went dark, but I've also never been this dark. I went a chestnut brown the year after I graduated high school, but I made the mistake of using permanent dye, which kept me pretty brassy for a year. This black, though . . . It's not bad.

I run my hands through my glossy post-dye hair in front of a vanity mirror that sits at the end of the upstairs hallway. I love the feeling of my hair after dyeing it. You need the right products to keep up the feel and health of your hair in the days and weeks after dye, but right after . . . That's the sweet spot. My mom always advised me against going darker, claiming it would drain me of my natural colouring. But as I stare at myself in a totally not vain way, I can't help but note how the dark hair with the vaguely blue undertones seems to pull out notes in my skin I haven't seen before. It also pulls out the subtle green glints in my hazel eyes. I find myself smiling at my reflection until I bite back the grin. I can almost hear Iris hyping me up in my mind.

I step back into Theo's room, basically the only place in the house, aside from Emma's room, with good lighting. I stand by the windows that face the front of the house, pouring in light from the setting sun, and pull out my phone. I snap a golden hour photo and send it to Hanna with the caption, "New hair. Who dis?"

My phone buzzes before I get a chance to stuff it into my back pocket.

Hanna: OMG OMG YOUR HAIR!!

And then . . .

Hanna: Girl, where are you?? Is that his bedroom?? ARE YOU IN HIS BEDROOM?? DID YOU DYE YOUR HAIR WITH HIM?? Do you know how much I ship this relationship omg

I giggle and debate sending more photos of my whereabouts. Those thoughts jar away when I hear Theo and Emma talking downstairs. I can't tell what they're saying, but notes of excitement in Emma's voice get me curious. I slip my phone into my back pocket, Hanna's questions ignored. A little mystery will do her good. I smooth my hand along Theo's dog-printed comforter and wonder, not for the first time, if it was his choice or Emma's. The little silhouettes of what seem to be golden retrievers in Fair Isle lines make me smile. The cream and deep red of the comforter ties in with the light wooden furniture, framed photos of Emma at varying ages, and dark walls. I don't know how it all works out, but it feels classy, cozy, kind of like a cabin. I could see Theo moving to a forested area away from the city and suburbs if the rest of his family weren't all settled around here.

I slink out of his hardwood-floored room and sink my feet into the shag carpet of the hallway. His house is so mismatched, but so obviously full of love and memories that it doesn't matter. I head down the stairs and am greeted by Rocket at the bottom. He licks my hand then falls into step next to me, thumping his tail against my legs as we walk.

A large mixing bowl, vanilla cake mix, Betty Crocker chocolate icing, sprinkles, candles, and a twelve-cup muffin tin greet me in the kitchen. Emma stands on a stool in front of the island, purple-streaked hair pulled back into a ponytail, where all the ingredients are laid out. I open my mouth, but I've been suddenly struck with the inability to speak.

Theo's hands wrap around my waist from behind and he whispers to me, "I wanted to do something special for Iris's birthday. After you told me, I went and grabbed some stuff at Shoppers. I hope that's all right."

I turn in his arms and nod. Tears come to my eyes and I'm not quick enough to blink them away this time. If I'm honest with myself, this birthday has fucked me up. My birthday in January fucked me up. I'm older now than Iris ever will be. She only got two months of twenty-five. I've had almost a whole year. Theo wipes my tears away with such gentleness that more fall. I laugh wetly and kiss him.

"I get to make cupcakes with Emma," I say, and I pretend not to notice my voice cracking. "Of course that's all right."

Chapter Twenty-Seven

I can't bring myself to look at the email. I've been sitting on the couch, staring at my phone for longer than what would be acceptable to most people. It's not out of the blue or unexpected. It's my doing. And yet, here I am, totally paralyzed by the thought of actually opening it and going any further.

The TV drones on in the background. I don't know what time it is or how long I've been sitting here, but it must be for a bit considering my mom has already gone upstairs, a fact I didn't realize until my dad moved in my peripheral vision. I draw my eyes away from my phone as Dad pushes himself up from the depths of his reclining armchair. He walks to me and places a hand on my shoulder.

"You know, Mom does really like your hair," Dad says, and it's so completely the last thing on my mind that I laugh.

"Well, she has a funny way of showing it."

When I came home on Saturday, two things happened. First, Mom stopped dead, mid-speech, and stared at me. I tried to get her to speak to me, but she stood there frozen, just staring, until she ran off upstairs. Dad complimented me and told me we matched now, while I tried not to look too confused. I pushed Mom's reaction out of my mind and went to my room where I sat down with my rediscovered confidence and did the second notable thing: I wrote an email to the Head of the Vocal Department, aka my former professor.

"Has she not said anything about it since Saturday?" Dad asks.

I place my phone facedown on the leather arm of the couch and angle my body so I can see my dad's face. "She has not."

He sighs and comes around to the front of the couch. He hesitates for a moment, then sits. I draw my knees to my chest, watching a pained emotion create creases next to his eyes. He pops his glasses up to rub below them.

"Can I be very honest for a minute?" he asks, and I nod. "With your hair like that . . . You look so much like Iris."

I take a sharp breath at her name. I can't remember the last time he's said it. Even yesterday, on her birthday, no one mentioned her.

"I kind of like that," I whisper. And it's true. I caught a glimpse of myself in the mirror last night and for a moment I thought I was seeing a ghost. Iris and I definitely looked related, but not exactly the same. But with the dark hair, I can see her in my face in places I hadn't before. "It's a nice reminder."

"It is," Dad agrees, a small smile on his lips. "And your mom thinks it suits you, as well. It was just a shock. We didn't expect you to come home with dyed hair, let alone hair that very much looks like her natural colour. Even though you're much taller and not extremely petite like her, for the briefest second, it was like she was here again.

A ghost of the past. It made zero sense, but for that second, I thought Iris had come to say hi for her birthday."

I don't know what to say to his candour. It's all I've wanted for the past two years, but now I don't know how to react. Instead of saying anything, I unfold myself from my corner of the couch and launch myself at my dad. He opens his arms immediately, as if he was waiting this whole time for me to hug him. We hold on to each other, listening to the sound of our breathing until we both subconsciously pull away.

"Do I tell you I love you enough?" Dad asks, that same pained expression pinching his features.

"Of course you do."

"Good. I always wonder if Iris knew."

"She knew. We all know. You made a garden of this family, and she loved you so much that she continued on with that tradition. She knew. You only left her room to see Poppy when she was dying." My voice breaks and I swallow the tears. "She knew."

He heaves a prolonged sigh as he gets off the couch. "Good. Good. I hope you never forget that."

"I won't," I say.

"And I hope you go back to singing."

I don't respond to his words. I let him walk away as the air slowly fades from my lungs. I eye my phone on the arm of the couch as if it's a bomb about to detonate. My feelings about singing are complicated and so intricately entwined in Iris. I want to restart my life. I can't continue on at the pub now that I know how desperately unhappy I am there, but I've come to realize that singing was not my thing. It was Iris's.

She was absolutely shit at singing and could not carry a tune, no matter how hard I tried to get her to learn. Forget me trying to teach her piano or guitar. She couldn't get it. But she lived through me doing all those things. She was always in my corner, letting me know I could be the next big singer-songwriter that I wanted to be. But as I re-emerge from the haze that's enveloped me for the past two years, I can't help but wonder if that was ever my dream.

When I sold my first song, I was over the moon. The joy I felt was a high I wanted to chase for the rest of my life, but then I got a different opportunity.

I wonder if I gave up on my real dream to follow someone else's.

But what does that mean now as I try to get back to the music? What does it mean now that I've started writing love songs again? Where do I go from here? Do I finish what I've started, or do I go for something else?

I pick up my phone and find the email I've been avoiding all day. I rid it of its ominous blue dot when I click on it. I see my name in the first line and close my eyes. I can do this. I've done it before. I aced it before. There is absolutely nothing that should stop me from being able to read this email.

And yet . . .

I open my eyes and swallow the anxiety, the fear, and every single emotion I already have on the line anticipating every possible word that could be in here. All I have to do is read the email. I don't have to do anything other than that. It doesn't mean I have to sing again or go back to school. It doesn't mean I have to dive headfirst into the realm of everything Iris wanted me to be. It's just a step.

It's so lovely to hear from you again, Magnolia.

Students come and go through here, but I do wonder when some disappear without warning. You were one of those for me. I always wondered. Unfortunately, I didn't know the circumstance surrounding your decision to withdraw. I would have loved to talk with you while you were mourning, though I understand it is presumptuous of me to assume you would want to at that time. I want to express my deepest condolences in the situation. I lost my brother at a young age as well and I have taken that with me throughout my life. If you'd like to speak about that, please do not hesitate to reach out.

In regards to the program, I can't automatically offer you your old spot, especially not at this point in the semester. I would, however, like to speak with you in person so we can further discuss this and your plans. If this is something you're interested in, let me know and we can pick a time.

All the best!

Arielle Forester

   I exhale and feel like an idiot for waiting all day to read this. Of course it wouldn't be anything automatic, and I shouldn't be surprised that she wants to talk to me personally. I sit there in the flickering light of the television, willing myself to write back.

   But I don't.

Chapter Twenty-Eight

"God, you look good," Theo mutters against my neck as I finish putting on my Morticia makeup.

I consider a few things: the odds of Emma resurfacing from her bathroom where she's becoming Wednesday and the odds of Poppy waking up from her pre-trick-or-treating nap, plus how badly I'll screw up my makeup, before I decide not to jump on him. But I do decide that my lipstick is not worth it. I can always reapply. I turn in his arms and my lips draw to his like a magnet. I can feel the unexpressed love I have for him coursing through my veins coming out through this kiss. His body leans into mine, hands braced on the counter behind me.

I pull back and smirk. "You look good with red lips."

I laugh as he hastily wipes the back of his hand over his mouth. I couldn't convince Theo to shave, so he's just Gomez with a beard now. Which is admittedly not as good as original Gomez. I fix my lips in the mirror, then briefly meet Theo's eyes. His trail along the dress that clings to each one of my curves. Theo and Emma convinced me that the lace dress was perfect, and if I'm being honest, the way he looked at me when I tried it on at the thrift store kind of sold me. When I brought it home, all I had to do was shorten the pooling sleeves just slightly, and now, I just had to use some boob tape to make sure the neckline didn't stray a bit too far.

"It's a shame you have to cover this up with a coat when we go out," Theo says, once more finding his hands on my hips.

"Promise you can have some fun with it later tonight," I say with a hand on his chest, then slink past him into his room.

Poppy sits in the centre of Theo's bed in her striped shirt, casually talking to her stuffed bear that used to be Iris's. Her costume is far more low key than the rest, but she still makes a good baby Pugsley. The moment she sees me, she drops the bear and scrambles to the edge of the bed. My eyes grow wide because I know she's about to launch herself right off like she does with everything, but this bed is higher than what she's used to. And, come to think of it, I'm not even sure how she got up there. I glance at the makeshift bed we'd made for her on the floor, now torn apart, pillows and blankets thrown about the room.

"Poppy!" I yell as she throws herself off the bed trying to get to me.

I lunge for her, but Theo gets there first, grabbing her by the foot. She giggles as she hangs upside down and I'm pretty sure I almost have a heart attack. My heart pounds against my rib cage, my hand going to my chest.

"Jesus," I whisper as Theo lowers her to the floor. "That was some kind of ninja reflex."

Theo laughs. "It's the dad reflex. Our one useful superpower is catching children the moment before they fall to their doom."

Poppy's giggles continue to bubble out of her as she decides she has a new favourite word. "Doom. Ha ha."

I roll my eyes and scoop Poppy into my arms. Theo turns off the light in the master bathroom before he heads to the bathroom Emma has claimed as her own. He knocks on her door that's open just a crack.

"You ready in there?" he asks.

Emma opens the door fully and frowns. Her hair hangs in meticulous long braids against her black dress. My hair has faded to a brown similar to Emma's. In hindsight, we dyed it too early, but maybe it works better this way. I grin.

"Oh, wow, you make the perfect Wednesday!" I exclaim.

She breaks from her well-rehearsed character and a grin about as wide as mine spreads across her face. "Thank you! It's good, isn't it? I wore something different to school with one of my friends, but I really wanted to be Wednesday. Can we take pictures? I'll just hide my arm behind you, okay?"

"You're not hiding your arm," Theo says. "It's a part of you and it's a memory you'll want to have later on."

Emma pouts. "I'm never going to want to remember *this*. And come on, Dad, Wednesday never broke her arm!"

Theo shrugs. "You don't know that. Plus, a broken arm could make Wednesday even more Addams-y. Broken bones are kind of spooky, right?"

He turns to me and I debate my answer. On the one hand, I never want to disagree with someone's parenting, especially not someone I want to continue seeing. But on the other hand, if she's not comfortable with it, I wouldn't force her. My brief hesitation speaks louder than an answer, and Emma sees it first.

"See! She disagrees!"

"Let's take both kinds of pictures," I scramble for the right answer. "That way you can have both sets of memories."

This placates both Hennessys. We head downstairs where Rocket immediately starts barking at the hand glued to Theo's shoulder. Poppy turns into my neck and I whisper assurances in her ear. Theo bends to Rocket's level and lets him sniff then gently gnaw on the hand until he somehow decides it's not a threat anymore. Apparently, a creepy hand is more threatening to Rocket than turning him into Cousin Itt. He'd had zero problem with us strapping a top hat and sunglasses on top of his head.

"Good boy," Theo says and snaps on Rocket's leash. "Everyone ready to go?"

We all mutter our agreement as we fumble around for our coats, shoes, stroller, and trick-or treat-bags. I shoot Theo a thumbs-up once we're all cozy in our coats and Poppy is buckled into the stroller. Even with the nap, I know she won't last long.

Theo turns on the string of Christmas lights inside his pumpkins and grabs a cauldron full of candy on his way out the door. The last to exit, I close the door and lock it behind me, then throw the keys to Theo once he places the cauldron down on a chair next to a handwritten sign Emma made letting kids know to only take one.

"Off we go!" Theo announces.

As expected, Poppy falls asleep three streets later. A combination of fresh air and being past her bedtime does her in. I cover her with her fuzzy pink blanket as we walk on. Theo and I walk just behind Emma as she chats busily with a friend of hers. The friend, who I assume she matched at school, is dressed as a jockey. She wears riding pants and boots, with a The Ranch branded T-shirt underneath a peacoat that's been styled to resemble a professional equestrian. Her hair back in a ponytail and the iconic black helmet tie the look together.

At an intersection, Emma hangs back from her friend while she crosses with her mother. Emma looks down at the shoes she was so proud to wear for Wednesday, almost as though she's holding back tears. I remove my hand from Theo's grasp and catch Emma's back, guiding her across the street.

"You all right?" I ask her.

"I'm fine," she says, and I can't tell if the frown is part of her costume or if she genuinely can't hide the emotion she's feeling.

I lick my lips, unsure about my place in her life, but I know Theo worries about her in the wake of her accident.

"Did I hear that right?"

"Hear what?"

"It sounded like your friend was talking about horseback riding and how she made a new friend there. Are you feeling a little left out?"

Emma doesn't say anything, just steels her gaze ahead of us. I let the conversation drop. She seems content with me just walking with her, until we reach the other side of the street.

"No, I'm fine."

I hadn't expected her to respond, and her defensiveness makes me wonder. It makes me feel as though there's more she wants to say, but she hasn't figured out the words yet.

"Your dad told me you're a little worried about riding

again," I say as we walk up toward the next block of houses. "Is that true?"

"I don't want to ride horses anymore," she states, but her chin wobbles.

"Are you sure? I mean, sometimes we have accidents and shi—stuff happens that makes it scary to go back to something again, but if you love it enough, you have to try. You know, literally get back on that horse."

Emma shakes her head. "I don't want to hurt myself again."

"It's a risk you take with anything. But the more you do it and the more you practise, the less of a chance you'll have another fall. We won't know that until you actually try again. And remember, I got back on stage after I broke my arm." I wink.

"Yeah, I guess," she says, and from her tone I can tell it's something she's already heard before, but then she shocks me. "I miss my friends. And the horses. So maybe."

She runs away to catch up with her friend at an extremely well-decorated house. Fog crawls out the front door, flashes of light spark along the ground within the smoke while a speaker plays thunderous music.

Theo stands behind me, a questioning look on his face. It takes me a moment to realize that the look is not directed at the house, but at me. He bites his bottom lip with slightly narrowed eyes.

"What?" I ask.

"Nothing," he huffs, but it's haughty and hides something. We walk in uncomfortable silence as Emma returns from the spooky house, shouting gleefully with her friend. The silence boils until the next house. "That was a really great speech you gave Emma. She seems to have thought about it more than anything I've said to her. I just . . . I guess I wish it was more than just words for you."

A chill goes down my spine and I stand perfectly straight. My voice comes out small. "What do you mean?"

"You told her shit happens and you have to get back on the horse eventually. I've been telling her that for weeks, and it's great she's hearing someone else saying that. But what does that mean to you as someone who hasn't gotten back on the horse?"

My brain can't form a sentence. My heart drops into my stomach. "I—I'm trying."

"You are?" he asks, eyebrows shooting up. His words aren't malicious, but each of them feels like a stab in the chest. "I mean, I know you are but . . . I'm sorry for how this sounds. I'm not trying to be mean, but"—he leans in closer to me to whisper, and I have to stop myself from flinching back because I know the next thing he says is going to break me—"don't you think that's a little hypocritical?"

"Excuse me?" I say, because hell yeah, that hurt, but it also struck a very real nerve.

"You're telling her to do something you can't do."

"I'm trying!" I repeat, but when I say it this time, it's a yell. A few heads turn our way. I don't care. "You're telling her the same thing. Does that make you a hypocrite?"

Theo blinks, trying to understand my logic. "No?"

"You wanted to be a doctor your whole life and you're not one now. You didn't get back on the horse. You did something else. Are you a hypocrite?"

"That was completely different."

"Was it?" I shriek. Emma and her friend jog back from the last house and hurry onto the next. Her friend's mom eyes us warily. I swallow my words until Emma is on a porch. "Please tell me how a change of plans makes me a hypocrite and not you."

"Because you didn't choose to change yours. You just dropped it." He sighs and closes his eyes. When he opens them, they're softer, apologetic, but I'm open and raw. "I shouldn't have brought it up right now, but Magnolia, look at me honestly and tell me you want to work at that pub. Tell me honestly that you've made an effort and you're trying to make things better for yourself. I can't be the only thing working in your life."

My eyes fill with tears. Not because he's wrong, not because he hurt me, not because I am so desperately unhappy with everything except him in my life. But because I can't tell him any of that. All my efforts are half-assed and futile. And I'm so damn terrified of what moving on looks like.

I shake my head. "No," I say. It's all I can manage. I shift his grip from Poppy's stroller and maneuver it away. I turn from him. "Tell Emma I had to leave because of Poppy or something."

Theo calls out to me. He reaches for my arm, but I disappear behind a group of trick-or-treaters and I'm gone before either of us realize what just happened to us.

Chapter Twenty-Nine

My bedroom door slams against the wall, and I'm half tempted to check for a dent in the pale yellow plaster. But I don't. I don't have the energy, and this shouldn't come as a surprise to anybody considering I haven't left my bed since coming home from Halloween two nights ago.

"Okay," Hanna says as she launches herself onto my bed, trapping the comforter around me. "Let's get this pity party started."

In spite of myself, I laugh. "How do you know it's a pity party?"

"Because you blew off work last night, and since it's 6:30 p.m., I'm pretty sure you blew it off tonight as well. You won't answer my texts. I've heard more from your boyfriend over the past day and a half than I have from you. And a little birdie shaped like Poppy tells me you're sick, so . . ."

She throws several brown paper bags at me. I flinch at the first, then draw the blankets over my head as the rest come.

"What the hell?" I say, muffled through my blanket pile.

Hanna rustles through the bags. "You did this for me when I broke up with that asshole in university, so I'm doing it for you now. But, like, we need to talk because you shouldn't break up with Theo."

I pull the blankets down and sit up. Hanna's eyebrows rise as she takes in my appearance. My hair hangs tangled on my shoulders and I'm wearing one of Theo's shirts. Admittedly, a very pathetic look to get caught in. I blush and look down at the tray Hanna's assembling. We have an array of French fries from different fast-food restaurants: McDonald's, Popeyes, Wendy's, A&W, Burger King, and Mary Brown's. When Hanna had a massive blow up, rip-up-your-ex's photos, burn-his-things breakup in first year university, I showed up at her dorm with French fries. We pigged out until the dull throb of her heartache lessened as our stomachs became full.

Tears come to my eyes as I take in the gesture. "Thank you," I say and reach for a fry.

She smiles as if it's nothing, but I see the worry behind it. "What the hell happened, dude?"

I pause, a limp fry dangling from between my pinched fingers. I stare at the sheet music I'd attached to the wall in front of my bed back in high school, trying to form a coherent thought for what I'm feeling. How do you explain to someone how hurt you are when you know the person who hurt you is right?

"Theo messaged me again. He said he couldn't get a hold of you, and he knew he'd kind of been an ass. But I have no context for that. What happened? Why is he apologizing and why aren't you talking to him?"

I glance down at my phone. I've been avoiding everyone, not just Theo. I don't know how to get my life together, especially when the one person I thought believed in me apparently doesn't. He thinks I'm a hypocrite because I can't find a way to get back to myself. I thought I was doing a good job of that with him, but I've come to realize I'm extremely good at pretending. My phone lights up and we both look down at it.

"Do you know you have seven messages from him?"

I swipe my phone up off the bed and place it facedown on my end table. "I know. Those are new ones. There's more where they came from."

"Jeez, Magnolia, what happened? What is going on? I've never seen you like this, let alone over a guy."

I run a hand through my hair and take a deep breath. "Don't you think that's weird? My sister died and I was fine. But God forbid I have an argument with some guy."

"I don't think it's weird," Hanna muses. She grabs a handful of fries and if someone could chew thoughtfully, she does it in this moment. "And Theo's more than some guy to you. I just think . . . Your response to bad things happening has always been running. Even before Iris, if you had a loss, you ran. You'd go travel or you'd put all your focus into something else. I think, maybe, right now you're finally letting yourself feel, and that's why whatever he said feels so awful. It's not just his words, it's all of it crashing down around you."

"How am I supposed to stop that?" I whisper.

"You're not supposed to stop it. You're supposed to feel it so you can process it and move on." She grabs hold of my hand and my chin trembles. "What did he say?"

"I told his daughter she should try going back to horseback riding and not let fear stop her from moving on," I say and start laughing because I know how goddamn ridiculous that advice is coming out of my mouth. "He heard me say that and told me it was a little hypocritical of me to give advice I can't follow, and you know what? He's right. What business do I have telling a little girl that when I can't even do it?"

Hanna shrugs. "Sometimes it's easier for kids to do the scary things than it is for us." She lets the words sit for a moment, then throws a fry at me. "And yeah, he's partially right, but he's also a dick for telling you that. He could have, like, gently asked how you were doing and if you were doing anything to get back on your horse. You don't just casually call someone a fucking hypocrite."

I give her a wry smile because I don't know what else to do or say. I shovel more French fries into my mouth, but it doesn't make me feel any better.

"Are you okay?" Hanna whispers. She runs a hand through her tousled curls and shakes her head. "Of course you're not. I just mean, this is more than him. Like yes, you had a fight, but this isn't just about the fight."

"I don't think I can be in a relationship right now. I don't think I can be with someone who has a kid because then there are two people I'll disappoint."

"Why do you think you're going to disappoint them?" she asks and shifts on the bed. She moves so she's sitting right next to me, and I rest my head on her shoulder.

"Haven't I already?"

"I think you underestimate yourself. They won't be disappointed unless you continue to ghost them. But, Magnolia, come on," she says and since she's using my full name, I know she's serious. "Theo really cares about you. He wouldn't be blowing your phone up if he didn't. He knows what you've been through. You told him all about

Iris, and I think it does mean something that he's the first one you opened up to about her. He knows you've had a rough go, and that's probably why he was upset the other day. He thinks you deserve more than you're settling for right now."

"I'm not settling for anything, I just don't know what to do."

"That's okay. Sometimes we don't know that and sometimes we don't have to."

"How do I figure that out?"

"You try."

I close my eyes and find tears streaming down my face. I let them fall, wetting the thin material of Hanna's shirt. She wraps her arms around me, and I cry against her. When my phone buzzes off the end table, Hanna reaches down for it. She reads Theo's latest text and turns it to me. Again, his words hurt me because of my own actions. It's as if he had ears on our conversation, and I don't know how to answer him because I don't know how to do what he and Hanna are asking for. I can pretend, but pretending is just that. It got me here.

Theo: I can't fix this if you don't want to try

Chapter Thirty

"Can you snap out of it, please?" Chloe says as I clean up a full glass of beer I just dropped. "I'm glad to have you back at work again, and I have been so glad since you came to rescue me from speed dating night, but Jesus, can you, like, be good?"

"Thanks," I mutter from the floor. "Very considerate."

"Sorry, I'm not trying to be inconsiderate. I just miss the old Magnolia."

I straighten with a huff, dustpan full of glass shards, and refrain from telling her I miss that too. Why the fuck would I not miss when I was happy? I walk past her, behind the bar where the garbage is, and dump the glass in. My coworkers have given me a wide berth over the past few days. A few asked me what was up, but after the first shrugged-off attempts, everyone just accepted I wasn't in the mood and needed space.

Chloe keeps trying, though.

"I get it. Breakups suck. But you can't let it get you this down."

I reattach the dustpan to the broom, stash it in the

closet by the break room, and swap it for a mop. I still don't know if Theo and I broke up. I guess the fact that I haven't spoken to him in seven days kind of says something . . . But I also hope my stupidity doesn't ruin us, and I can come back to him and pretend like nothing happened.

Pretend. I laugh to myself.

"What is going on with you lately?" Chloe asks.

I lean against the bulletin board outside the break room. Papers crunch behind me and I focus on the sound so I don't laugh or cry or walk right out the door. I push a dull faded brown lock behind my ear and finally look up at Chloe. Her arms are crossed over her chest and her full lips pout in a confused scowl.

"I don't know," I breathe. I shake my head. "I truthfully do not know what's going on with me. I think I'm doing some long overdue processing."

"Processing what?"

"Life. Love. Death . . . I guess I haven't really done that," I say and fiddle with the handle of the mop.

Chloe looks at me like I've sprouted an extra head. She lets out a pronounced and clearly exasperated sigh. I look down at the greyish strands of the mop and bite my lip to keep from laughing.

"Well, who the fuck even does that?"

I let the laugh bubble out. "I don't know. People who are far healthier than I am, I guess. I just want to feel better, Chlo."

I push past her and walk back to the puddle of beer I made. I haven't dropped a plate or a glass since my first week here. I learned the balance ropes quickly and kept my thoughts firmly placed on the job every time I was in. I guess that's my avoidance right there.

"Are you saying you're not healthy?" Chloe asks, popping up next to me as I mop.

I peek up at her under my lashes. "Uh, well yeah. Mentally, I'm not doing great."

"Who told you that? Was it that guy?"

"No, it was me. I'm more than aware of how I've been feeling lately and how this isn't new. At all. I subconsciously made a choice a while ago to not deal with the things that scare me, and that's why I'm stuck here. So I have to figure that out."

"Come to Asia with me."

I roll my shoulders as I straighten up again. The floor is wet, but at least it's not sticky. I stare at Chloe's impassive face, trying to judge whether she's serious. Her eyebrows merely raise as I study her. She's anticipating an answer I don't have. I walk back to the supply closet.

"I'm serious," Chloe says. Her face appears by my right side after I close the closet. I jump, not because I didn't expect her to follow me, but because she's so close to me. "I booked the trip. I'm leaving December 30. All you have to do is follow my itinerary and book the same places and flights. Think about how great it was when we met up in Europe. We could do that again!"

I close my eyes and think about bad decisions. I could say yes. I could agree to go and shirk my responsibilities once more. I could run.

"No."

"No?" Her hands go to her hips.

"I can't. I can't run off over and over again. It makes no sense to me anymore. I actually have to work on my life instead of running from it."

Chloe takes a step away from me and places a hand on her chest. From anyone else, I'd think it was dramatic. But I know she's genuinely offended. "Are you saying that's what I'm doing?"

"No. I'm saying that's what I would be doing. We're different people, Chlo. Travel invigorates you. It recharges you and makes you you. And I'm not saying I wouldn't love a vacation, but if I went anywhere right now, it wouldn't be a vacation. It would be me running from my feelings yet again, and I don't want to do that. I love you, but I can't go."

Her hands fall to her sides and I'm certain she isn't going to answer me. She's one eye roll away from walking out on the conversation. "You can't do a lot of things lately, it seems. What can you do?"

I didn't expect her to ask that. I open my mouth, but no sound comes out. The fact is, there are so many things I won't let myself do right now because they would be me avoiding any progress I could possibly make. But I don't know what I *can* do. I know if I tell her that, she'll walk away and won't talk to me for the rest of our shift. Maybe that wouldn't be such a bad thing, but I'm not sure I can take another person's disappointment in me right now.

"I can—"

"Can the two of you stop having a chat and get back to work already!" Andy yells from inside the break room.

I couldn't be more grateful for his interruption. Chloe and I scramble back into the noisy pub and head in two different directions.

Chapter Thirty-One

I sit in the Bug in the school parking lot and think of nothing other than a string of expletives. If Poppy weren't in the backseat, I would absolutely have a moment of banging on the steering wheel, screaming *fuck* at the top of my lungs.

> **Magnolia:** I'm pretty sure my mom is trying to pimp me out

Hanna: I lolled in a patient's room at that. But WHAT??

> **Magnolia:** I'm chaperoning a field trip. Some parent cancelled last minute

Hanna: YOU BETTER TALK TO THEO

My lips quirk up. I'd be lying if I said I wasn't thinking about him. Mostly because I'm hoping he's not coming on the trip. The last contact I had with him was a text saying I needed space to figure things out. And that was a week ago. He accepted but obviously wasn't happy about it. He offered his help if I needed it and, fuck, I want to take his help so bad but at this point I don't even know what I need.

I slide out of the car when I see the school bus pull up in the front driveway. I gather Poppy and all her items in my arms. I lean against the door of the car. Someone a few spots over is doing the same. Before I have a chance to see who the person is, Poppy lets me know with a squeal.

"Hello," Theo says as I turn to face him.

"So, I guess my mom knew you were coming," I say and the dry, almost bitter tone in my voice shocks me.

Theo's eyes widen for the briefest second, but he covers that with a shrug. "Maybe. I didn't know you'd be here. I'm not trying to disrespect your wishes or anything."

"I know," I say with a laugh. "You don't have a disrespectful bone in your body."

"I don't know. Some would say that calling someone a hypocrite is pretty disrespectful." I stiffen and he notices. He changes subjects. "I like your hair."

I run a hand through my much shorter locks. I went to a hairdresser so they could freshen up my blonde, too tired of seeing the mousy brown the hair dye left me with. My waves now hang just below my chin, choppy and layered, overall much brighter.

"Thank you," I say.

"We twins!" Poppy exclaims, repeating what my mom had said the second I got home from the salon. I have a mini me once again with those matching blonde ringlets.

I smile, then push off the car. Students begin filing out the front doors. I close my eyes and steel myself for the next few hours with two grade-two classes: sixty-three kids and six adults. Mom walks out with her class and arranges them into different groups. Once she's happy with their little lines, she turns and spots me. I raise a free hand and see Theo do the same a few paces ahead of me.

"Here," Mom says and reaches for Poppy when I stand

next to her. "I'll take Poppy for today and add her into my group. It'll make it easier for you to watch your kids since I'm used to multitasking."

"Oh, okay," I say and hand over the diaper bag as well. I wrap my arms around myself, suddenly chilled.

Theo steps closer to me and gently touches my waist. He shrinks back, but not before I feel the warmth from his skin leave me. It sends a shiver through my body. I glance at the ground to hide my blush.

"All right, second graders, listen up!" Miss Ayaz addresses the children. She's in her late 20s, with the chicest style and most perfect inky black eyeliner. "You each have your group and your chaperone. Please stick with each other once we get to the rink. If you have any issue, talk to your chaperone."

She goes on to explain who is in whose group. The three parents volunteering are in charge of their child's group, while the teachers get a group from their class, and I get the rejects. I introduce myself to the kids and let them know a fun fact about myself because it's what everyone else has done. They seem amused when I tell them I'm a singer, a fact that surprises me, and evidently surprises my mother and Theo.

We file onto the bus. The adults hang back as the kids climb in. I stand off to the side and watch silently, arms still wrapped around myself. My bones feel tired and weary, and I haven't even fallen on an ice rink a million times yet. I try to make sense of my gut reaction that the most fun fact about myself is that I'm a singer. Even though I'm not and haven't really identified with that since Iris died. I also try to make sense of the fact that immediately after I said that, it felt wrong.

"Magnolia, come on," Mom says and waves me onto the bus.

I'm the only one still outside. I hope the other mom on the trip likes Theo and sat beside him, much as that also makes my stomach turn, or that Mom wants to sit with both me and Poppy. I walk up the steps and turn, assaulted by the vaguely rubber scent of the bus, and find the only empty seat next to Theo. He absently stares out the window and has the good grace to look the slightest bit embarrassed. I sigh as I sink down into the seat.

Theo shifts farther toward the window, but seeing as he's a broad, bulky man and we're both tall, there's no way to avoid our thighs touching. Electricity jumps between us. This is the exact opposite of space.

"Sorry," Theo says. The tips of his ears flame. He stares straight ahead at the bench in front of us.

I bite back a smile and focus on my hands clasped together in my lap for the remainder of the bus ride. Or, at least, I try to. I've forgotten how bumpy bus rides are, and every lurch in the road sends me careening into Theo.

"Sorry!" I say as my elbow connects with his ribs.

He laughs it off and there is something so magical about it that I feel my resolve slipping. Maybe I'm mad and confused and hurt and anxious about the future, but maybe I don't have to be alone to figure all of that out.

I turn to Theo. He's looking everywhere except at me. I want to tell him I love him, or that maybe he was right, or that maybe I don't want space like I thought I did. I want to say all these things all in a rush, but the bus stops before I can, and the noisy chatter of excitable children comes to a high.

Miss Ayaz stands at the front of the bus and holds her

hand up in the air, waiting for the kids to quiet. In a matter of seconds, the bus is silent. She smiles.

"I know that was a very short trip, but we have arrived! The six of us are going to get off first, then you can all follow, find your chaperone, and we'll all head in together. Sound good?"

The kids yell their agreement and Miss Ayaz nods, then gestures for the adults to leave. I swing my legs into the aisle and stand, having lost all my nerve. I now no longer want to be near Theo. Theo grabs the seat in front of him and pulls himself up. A muscle in his arm jumps. Something about it gets me and I have to look away. Walk out.

I stand on the curb in front of the bus and wait for my group of kids. My gaze strays to Theo in his spot a few feet away from me. His eyes meet mine without hesitation. I swallow hard and tear my eyes away. I plaster a smile on my face so no one notices the tension coursing between us.

We can't keep our eyes off each other. We stay on opposite sides of the rink when we can. We listen to the lithe former figure skater tell the kids how to skate, me by the entrance, Theo by the rink. Our eyes keep meeting and each time they do, something deep within me stirs. As I put on my skates, a flash of forest-green plaid and jean passes me. I pause with my hands on the laces and let the heat envelope my body for a moment, a truly odd sensation at an ice rink. Theo sits at the end of the same bench and my breath catches when his icy eyes bore into mine. My chest flames. Theo winks and my body feels as though it could burn down.

"Magnolia!" Emma calls and snaps me out of whatever thing Theo and I had going on more violently than if another child came up to me. "Look! I got my cast off!"

"Oh, good!" I say, clearing my throat and trying hard to snap out of my Theo daze, especially in front of his kid. "That's so great! That means you're allowed to skate, right?"

She side-eyes Theo and I laugh. "I would. But Dad doesn't want me to."

"Come on, Dad!" I call to Theo before I can stop myself. I flush, then quieter I say, "If she wants to skate, let her skate."

Theo just stares as if that's an obvious conclusion, then mutters dryly, "We don't need any more broken bones."

"Are you here to make sure she doesn't skate?" I raise my eyebrows to challenge him. "I'm sure you were skating at her age. Hockey has to start somewhere, right?"

He pauses on his laces, much like I did, and scowls at me. I can't tell if it's playful or if he genuinely doesn't want Emma on the ice. I finish lacing up my skates. Emma skips away to her dad, and they have a muffled conversation. I take a breath and stand. A glance over my shoulder leads to more intense eye contact. Emma has run off with a friend, skates in hand. I smirk and step onto the ice.

I'm not a good skater by any means. Skating is not like riding a bike. It's not something you do as a little kid so fluidly and remember twenty years later. I hold on to the railing around the edge of the rink and make a slow loop. My group fares much better than I do. One little girl in my group even does a spin in the middle of the ice. I join in on the brief applause for her, then go right back to holding on to the boards.

Kids zip past me and somehow this does not make me feel great about myself. I already feel just the slightest bit incompetent in life as a whole. Watching children excel at something you literally cannot do is extremely disheartening. A boy in Theo's group gets a little too close for comfort and I inadvertently push away from the wall.

"Fuck," I mutter under my breath.

I hold my arms out at my sides, desperately clawing at balance. My feet slide along the ice, but I have zero rhythm in skates, on slippery ground, so one leg moves faster than the other. I careen forward and completely regret agreeing to come on this trip. My right foot picks at the ice. I trip. I'm falling forward and I know it's not a life-or-death thing, but I swear my life flashes before my eyes as the ice gets closer and closer.

Hands grasp me around my waist and stop my fall. They pull me upright against a chest I'm all too familiar with. My heart pounds and I'm certain it's half adrenaline, half Jesus-Christ-I'm-back-in-Theo's-arms.

"You really told my daughter to skate when you flounced out here and almost did a full-on face plant?" Theo bites out with a laugh.

I catch my breath, straighten, and look up at him. "Yes. I did. I never said *I* was any good."

He shakes his head, and his amused smile kills me a little. "You, Magnolia dear, are ridiculous."

"Thank you," I say with a nod. "I pride myself on it."

At the same moment, Theo and I realize I'm still plastered against his chest. We jump apart and I lose balance again. Theo's hand clasps around my wrist and steadies me. Then, suddenly, we're holding hands as he guides me to the edge of the rink again.

"All good?" he asks.

I nod, standing perfectly straight, my head the only inch of my body moving. Theo nods back and, with a look in his eye so close to pain that my soul aches, he turns and skates away.

Chapter Thirty-Two

Magnolia: Can you meet me outside the pub tonight before I work?

I stand in front of the pub, leaning up against the jagged, artistic brick at the end of the bank of windows. Seeing Theo at the rink stirred something in me, and evidently, it did the same for him. After he saved me from falling on my face and skated away, we both tried so hard to avoid each other's gazes that we wound up staring at each other more. All I could think of was leaving the ice and making out with him in one of the change rooms, but that didn't seem like the most appropriate reaction with fifty kids watching us. So we separated and continued our intense eye-contact game that made me feel like my insides were melting with every little glance and nearly burned me down on the bus ride home. I can only assume the other chaperones noticed our tension on that bus.

I texted him this morning before I thought to process yesterday's events or how I felt about my future.

I need to sort this out now.

"Hey," Theo says, shuffling up to me from a dark corner of the parking lot.

I smile and immediately pull him to me. My hands tangle in his hair as his lips crash into mine. I've been standing outside in the cold for fifteen minutes, the chill keeping the adrenaline in my veins at bay. But now his warmth overtakes my body. I throw myself into the kiss and I can tell from his passion and the way his hands find my waist, snake up under my suede jacket, and pull me tight against his chest that he's doing the same. Passion surges through me, settling in the pit of my stomach, thumping against my ribcage. Theo smells hot and fresh, with just a hint of spice, like he just showered. As I breathe him in, I finally notice his hair is damp beneath my fingers.

I laugh into the kiss and taste the smile on his lips. He pulls his face away from mine at the same moment he pulls me flush against him. I slide my hands from his hair to cup his face.

"Hey," I say.

He laughs. "Hey there, Mags."

Hearing my name on his lips, the only person in the world who uses that as my nickname, sends waves of happiness through me. I grin. I revel in the warmth of his arms for a moment before I launch into everything I have to say. I shoot my gaze downward so I don't lose myself in those damn eyes.

"Theo! Again?!" I say indignantly once I see he's wearing shorts.

"I came from work."

"You definitely don't wear shorts at work," I say, then pause. "Shouldn't you still be at work?"

He nods and smirks. "I probably should be. But I only had a half hour left and got a buddy to cover for me. Told them I had to go get the girl."

"You got her," I whisper, tucking myself against him. I stay that way for a moment, listening to his heartbeat before I pull away. His hands find their way to my shoulders and ghost their way down to entwine with my fingers. "First of all, I'm sorry."

"What? Why are you sorry?"

"For pushing you away."

Theo chuffs. "You had every right to push me away after what I said to you."

"The thing is," I say and squeeze his hands, "you weren't wrong. I do give advice I can't follow. I have been pretending everything's okay for over a year when it hasn't been. I run when I can't deal with life. And I did all that on Halloween."

"Yeah, but I was a dick."

I raise my eyebrows and nod. "You were a dick about it, yeah. But I could also argue that I'm kind of a dick too."

Theo shrugs. "Don't we all have a little bit of a dick in us?"

He can't keep a straight face and I burst out laughing as well. The remaining tension between us evaporates during our laughing fit. We hang on to each other, making love-drunk steps as our laughter comes to a crescendo.

"I'll agree to that too," I say once I've caught my breath. "But I just wanted to apologize and say thank you."

"Can I say the same to you?" he asks.

"Why?"

"I'm sorry I was a dick, and thank you for being you. The past two weeks have sucked for me because I haven't fucking seen you at all until yesterday. What I said was stupid and rash, even if you say it's true. I want you, Mags. I want you even if you're messy or a dick. I want to be on this journey with you even if it takes you two more years or forever to figure out. I want you."

"Fuck," I breathe and it comes out as a stream of foggy air. "That's so much better than what I was going to say."

He laughs. "I'm sure it's not. What were you going to say?"

"It's just . . . It's hard for me, I guess, and it has been for a really long time and I haven't really realized that. I've pushed it aside because I thought that's what everyone was doing, but by pushing it aside I've made myself more confused. I'm sorry for acting so childish and not talking to you after we fought. You struck a nerve and it hurt me because on some level, you were right. I didn't know how to say to your face that I haven't been helping myself. Everything I've done to try and help myself hasn't been fully thought out, and I haven't followed through on any of it. I guess that's where the thank you comes in. You've helped me process more about Iris's death and my shambles of a life in the last two months than anyone has in the last two years."

"That's a pretty good speech too."

Theo brings one of my frozen hands up to his lips. He kisses it softly then lets it fall back to my side. I smile at him, nearly on the verge of tears. I forgot in my mad desire to run that talking to him about all of this feels good. His lips quirk and soon, he's grinning. He leans in for a kiss but pauses when I hold up a hand to wave at Chloe. At first, he must think I'm stopping him from kissing me, and his eyebrows draw together.

"Hey, Chlo!" I call over to her.

Chloe freezes with her hand flat against the door, pushing it slightly ajar. Her eyes shift between me and Theo, and her hand comes up to shield her face and that one white streak. Theo stiffens. He drops my hands. His face, flushed pink from the cold, somehow goes pale. Chloe's shoulders shake as she sighs and stands unguarded at the door. She purses her lips as she makes bashful eye contact with Theo. It's a look I've never seen on her, and the rage burning behind Theo's eyes is one I've never seen on him either. Chloe slips inside and Theo turns to me, hands shaking, eyes mercifully closed.

"You know her?" Theo says, voice gruff as if it takes effort to form the words.

"Chloe? Yeah. She got me the job here after Europe."

"You went to Europe with her?"

"I— No, I met her there. What's going on? Why are you shaking?"

The laugh that escapes his lips is one I never want to hear again. It's so broken, so full of anger. He shakes his head as if he can't believe what's going on. When he finally looks at me again, I step back, colliding with the wall with an *oof*. His eyes have never looked so icy. They're not just blue in colour now—there's no life in them, just pure anger and sorrow.

"All this time and you've never once mentioned that you're best friends with Chloe Alastair." He spits her name like it's a curse.

"I'm definitely not best friends with her. Friends, sure. But we mostly just work together."

"You travelled with her. That's more than just work buddies, Magnolia. Fuck. I can't do this right now."

Theo turns away from me and takes long strides back to his car. I don't know what's going on. For a moment, all I can do is stand there and blink at his retreating form. Then something tells me to run. Follow him. I almost let him go once. I can't let him go again.

"Theo, wait!" I yell as I run to catch up with him.

He whips around to face me. Tears threaten to spill from his eyes, making the blue stand out more than normal. My mind frantically connects dots as the blue in his eyes reminds me of Emma's heterochromia, a genetic condition sometimes passed down from a parent who also has a genetic condition that causes pigmentation issues.

Chloe is Emma's mother.

"Shit," I whisper. "I swear I had no idea."

Theo shakes his head like he can't believe this. Or me. He wipes the back of his hand over his eyes and yanks the driver's side door open.

"I should have stayed at work," he says and slams the door on me.

The cold fully seeps into my bones as I step back and watch him pull out of the lot. Part of me wants to break down and cry, but it turns out that's a small part. The other part of me lets me stand there for only a few seconds before I pivot on my heels and barge into the pub. There are no events today. Just the usual Thursday-night crowd. Chloe isn't here and it almost makes me see red that she's intentionally not facing me. I can't hold back the eye roll, which is good, because I do hold back the scream.

I storm into the back of the pub, past the bar and the aprons and into the break room. Chloe isn't there either.

"Magnolia!" Andy calls. "Take off your coat and stay

awhile."

I do as I'm told with minimal complaint. I'm saving it for Chloe.

"Where's Chloe?" I ask.

Andy raises his eyebrows at the harshness of my voice, but I catch the brief quirk of his lips. One thing Andy likes about pub life is the drama and gossip, whether it's about our usuals or our coworkers.

"She went into the bathroom the second she got here. Suit up. You can catch her later."

I grab my apron off the hook. I'm sure Andy knows as well as I do that I'm not going to catch her later. I'm going to wait in front of that damn dingy bathroom stall that everyone I've ever worked with has done their best to avoid until Chloe gets her ass out. I pull my phone out of my back pocket as I wait for her.

> **Magnolia:** I'm so sorry
>
> **Magnolia:** I know you might not believe me but I really had no clue
>
> **Magnolia:** And that might not sound true because somehow I know she's Emma's mother but I swear I didn't. There's only one person in the world you'd react that way to
>
> **Magnolia:** Please believe me

I nearly text that I love him, but I'm not weaponizing that confession.

After I wait for ten minutes, I bang on the door. Not a light, polite knock for your friend. An angry, incessant pounding that's unignorable.

Chloe unlocks the door and walks out looking exactly

like she always does. Cool, unbothered, perfectly poised in a half slouch with deep-red lips. I stare at her and she does the same to me. Anger gives way to sadness over what she's put this man I love through.

"How could you?" I whisper.

She continues to stare at me in that levelled manner that gives nothing away. Then, she rolls her eyes so hard that I see only the whites for a split second. She pushes past me into the pub. I stand, open mouthed.

"Chloe! Are you serious? You're just going to walk away and say nothing?" I rush up to her and yank on her upper arm. Just as quickly, she forces herself out of my grasp. "Pretty ballsy move."

"Get the fuck out of my face," she says darkly. She takes a step toward me, somehow managing to make all five feet of herself intimidating. "If I wanted to talk to you about this, I would. But I don't. I don't talk to anyone about this. So you have two choices. You can drop it, or you can fuck off."

I keep her glare. My hands ball into fists at my sides and my teeth grind together. Her eyes send daggers and flames my way and I'm certain that if that were a superpower, I'd be dead right now. I've seen Chloe enact her death glare on disrespectful customers. Never on me.

"Chloe," I start. Because I just want to understand. I just want to know. "Why?"

"Fuck off, Magnolia."

Chapter Thirty-Three

I somehow manage to pull myself out of bed to attend Hanna's bridesmaid brunch on Saturday. Granted, I don't officially know it's a bridesmaid brunch, but I know. She wouldn't have brought her sisters and cousin out if it wasn't to ask all of us to be bridesmaids.

I arrive after everyone else is already seated. They look like an advertisement for basic autumn brunch, decked out in slouchy sweaters, dark makeup, and knee-high boots, gathered around the table with wine glasses waiting. And I'm no stranger to the vibe. I'm also here for wine and dressed in my own oversized cardigan. Hanna chose Symposium Cafe mostly because she's big on their sangria.

I slide into the end of the booth, next to one of Hanna's nursing friends, Sloane. Sloane, who I haven't seen in forever, always makes the best jokes and has the best hair advice. I have never not been jealous of her gorgeous, glossy chestnut-brown locks. She moves her purse onto the ground and smiles as I settle in.

"Sorry I'm late," I say.

Hanna meets my eyes, a silent question in them. I

furiously texted her block after block of text after I found out about Chloe until she called me to get the full rant. I hang somewhere between disbelief and sorrow over the events of the past few days. Theo still hasn't said anything to me. I smile and nod like a *Madagascar* penguin. She looks at me as though the conversation isn't over, but we have bigger fish to fry now.

I graciously accept wedding plans over whatever the hell kind of mess I've currently gotten myself into.

Hanna sits in the middle of the semi-circle booth, sandwiched between her sisters. Older sister Alicia on the right, next to Sloane, younger sister Kit on the left. Hanna is the middle sibling, but first to get engaged. With a two-year engagement ahead of us, though, Alicia could still take the marriage crown first. Anything's possible. Hanna's cousin Marlena sits next to Kit, with our high school friend Gigi rounding out the group. I inwardly whistle. Six bridesmaids. Does Drew even have six friends?

The pitcher of sangria arrives, and I reach for it first. I need something to take the edge off, though I have no intention of getting fully drunk, which I guess sangria is decent for. I pass it off to Sloane and it makes its way around the table. Hanna waits to make her speech until we've all ordered. I keep my thoughts focused on my forthcoming Belgian waffles and breakfast potatoes.

"I'm so glad you guys were all free today," Hanna says and smiles personably at each one of us. "I'm sure you all know why you're here."

Polite laughter passes between us. I fidget with the hem of my tank top and try to place where, exactly, my anxiety is coming from. I have no qualms against other people experiencing love while my heart feels like it's shattering, so I have zero idea why my skin is crawling.

Hanna dips below the table and pulls a large tote bag out when she resurfaces. It clatters onto the table and nearly upends her wine glass. Alicia reaches for it on reflex before it can topple. Hanna mouths a thank you, a glint in her eyes.

"Now that I've almost drenched the surprise . . . I have something for each of you guys."

Hanna passes floral-patterned boxes to each of us, our names printed on top in gold script. She nods and we collectively open them. Inside are three pink macarons, silver earrings tied into a knot with a little slip of card stock that reads, "I couldn't tie the knot without you," and a folded silken robe with crisp black lettering that reads *Bridesmaid*.

"Oh my God!" Alicia says and pulls out her robe with slightly different words. Her well-manicured hand with nails in the exact same shade as Hanna's goes to her chest. "You want me to be your maid of honour? I was so sure you'd pick Magnolia. This is so sweet."

"Well, no offence to Lia," Hanna starts.

"Absolutely none taken," I say to mixed laughter.

"But of course you would be, Alicia. You've been there for me through everything. I wouldn't dream of having anyone else standing up there with me." Hanna turns, a slight flush on her face. She grabs her younger sister's hand. "I love you too, Kit, but I could only pick one of you."

Kit shrugs. "It's cool. Maid of honour is too much work for me, anyway. Alicia will thrive in the role."

"It'll be your best role to date!" Marlena chimes in.

Alicia is an actress. I used to talk with her about the

artist's struggle when I had aspirations as well. I stare down at the bridesmaid box in front of me and feel the crashing realization of why today hurts.

Hanna grieved with me when Iris died, because she's my best friend and of course you do that for your best friend. But Hanna knew what it would be like to put herself in my shoes. Alicia and Hanna are only a year apart. They're best friends as much as I was with Iris.

Iris and I had a pact. We'd be each other's maids of honour no matter what. We just never accounted for the "no matter what" that included her dying before either of us got to that part.

"I cannot wait to dance with you at your wedding," Gigi says. She throws her hands up in the air as if demonstrating their future shenanigans. I force myself to laugh. "We just need some 'Dancing Queen' and boom."

Hanna beams. "It's going to be the best. I have such high expectations for my wedding. I'm sure you guys know it's two years from now. That's the only date we could get, and I would not compromise on this venue. So, keep your schedules clear for September 20, 2025!"

We murmur our agreement. Sloane takes out her phone and marks it in her calendar. I giggle, knowing Hanna won't let us forget if we tried. She's going to milk this for all its worth, throw all the parties, and celebrate the shit out of her relationship over the next twenty-two months. And she deserves to. I bite down on my lip. Though I'm beyond happy for her, I'm honestly not sure how long I have left until the dam breaks.

I swallow my overwhelm of emotion and pray that the glossiness in my eyes looks like happy tears. "Toast?"

"To the future Mr. and Mrs. Bennett!" Alicia cries.

We all raise our glasses and clink with each other, repeating Alicia's words.

Chapter Thirty-Four

After aimlessly driving for a few hours, I find myself in a graveyard after the bridesmaid proposal. I don't tell my parents where I'm going, mostly because I didn't have a clue until I pulled past the iron gates of the cemetery. I didn't tell them Theo and I probably broke up. I figured since I hadn't heard from him since he walked away that we were done for good this time. He hasn't answered any of my texts or calls. It's been absolute, infuriating silence. Silence I can't do anything about unless I show up at his doorstep, which I could have done now, but part of me doesn't want to see his sad, angry eyes. And I guess that's part of why my subconscious brought me here.

I stop in front of a line of headstones by the back corner of the cemetery. I haven't been here in almost two years, and I've only ever been here once, but I know exactly where to go. The wind blows my hair around my face the second I step out of the Bug. I reach into the backseat and find my winter hat with a tawny fuzz ball on top, and a picnic blanket. The hat tames my wild, slightly too short hair.

My body absently carries me to Iris's grave. The headstone sits in the centre of the row, three rows back from the forest that lines the cemetery. Fallen leaves crunch beneath my feet as I walk along the row. In a sea of grey stones, Iris's stands out in mahogany granite. You never want to consider what someone's headstone is going to look like, but I insisted two years ago that she have something like this. She always stood out in crowds. She needed to stand out in death too. Her death was a surprise and happened in winter, so we couldn't immediately put up a stone. At her funeral, a spike poked out of the ground of her plot bearing her name and time alive. I remember standing here, shaking, not knowing whether it was from the cold or my tears.

I lay the blanket out on the cool grass, intending to sit and talk to my sister, but I wind up lying down on it. I clasp my hands together and lay them over my belly button. Clouds pass in the pink and orange sky above me. The sun sets just behind her headstone. I close my eyes in the peace of rustling branches and birdsong. Tears slip silently down my cheeks.

"Iris," I whisper. "I don't know what I'm doing anymore."

I lie there and wait for some response from the universe, even though I know it won't come. I wipe the tear tracks from my face and take a shaky breath.

"Everything feels like it's falling apart. And I don't know what I want or why I'm here because I don't think you can help, but I just wanted to be near you. You always knew what to say. You always helped me fix my messes."

My hands press into my eyes. I will myself to stop crying, if only so I can sound less garbled as I speak to her. Even if no one else is around and no one else can hear me. I so desperately want her help, but I don't want her to see the mess I've become without her.

"I think I've somehow ruined my relationship. I had a boyfriend, did you know? And I think I loved him. I felt that magical thing you were always talking about. I never wanted him to let go of me any time I was in his arms. He's the best, but he's mad at me for something that isn't even my fault, and I don't know how to fix that. Because I get why he's so pissed off. I probably would be too if I was in his situation. You know what, I'm pissed at James. I get he was grieving after you died, but that still gives him no excuse to ditch Poppy. I wish he never did that. I wish he knew Poppy because she is just so beautifully you. So I understand why Theo is mad. Because I'm mad at my life and he must be too. To know that someone is missing out on loving someone . . . God, I miss you, Iris."

I curl my body around itself and open my eyes to Iris's grave. I reach out to touch the cold stone, expecting it to somehow be warm under my palm just like she used to be. My hand flinches back, startling me into further fervent cries. Through blurred eyes, I notice a lyric from "Iris" by the Goo Goo Dolls inscribed on her headstone. "Iris" remained her favourite song throughout her whole life, right from the moment Dad played it for her when she was four years old up to the moment she insisted on playing it the first time she held Poppy. A strangled cry exits my body.

I'd suggested the lyric about heaven. Seeing it engraved in stone breaks me that much more. I cry until I've run out of tears. Until my eyes hurt, my nose is red, my throat is dry, and the sun has gone down. With shaky breaths, I sit up. Cold has seeped into my veins but it doesn't matter. I've been here too long to care or to even feel it. I run my hands along the fleece royal-blue plaid of the blanket and wrap it around myself.

I imagine looking into Iris's eyes as I stare at her headstone. I see her dark eyes and hair, the dimples in her cheeks when she smiles, her uncannily well sculpted eyebrows, those perfect teeth from the braces she needed and I never had. I swear to God she grins at me.

"I miss you so damn much. I wish you were still here. Sometimes I wish it were me who went instead of you." I whisper it all quickly, my voice grating on every syllable. "I've been so lost without you. I wish you could fix my problems like you used to, but I guess I'm realizing that I have to learn how to do that eventually."

I bite my trembling lip. What would she do if she knew what I've been thinking lately?

"I don't want to be a singer, Iris. I don't know what I want to do, but I don't think I want that. Part of me feels like I have to go back to the program just to finish it, but I don't want to be a singer. I think . . . I think that was your dream for me, and I never really saw it. I know I can sing. I know that if I busted my ass as much as you made me, I could probably figure out a way to do that, but I don't think I ever wanted to. I wanted to write. I wanted to make music. The happiest I've ever been was when I sold that song. And it really fucking sucks because now that's tainted. Every time I hear it, I kind of want to puke because it makes me think about you and how much more you wanted for me. But what if I don't want that?"

The words echo around me. What if I don't want that? What do I do now?

As if saying the words out loud are magic, a weight lifts off me. I breathe in the crisp night air and nod.

"That's okay, isn't it?"

Chapter Thirty-Five

"Chloe put in her resignation?" I ask Andy in the break room that Wednesday after I find her two-weeks' notice in a stack of papers.

I turn to face him. He sits on the disgusting couch, sipping a milkshake through a fancy straw, casually scrolling on his phone. Milkshakes are the new addition to the menu and Andy cannot complain, especially considering it was his idea. He grabs one every shift now.

"Hmm?" Andy says. He looks up from his phone and stares at the paper I'm holding uncomprehendingly. "Oh! Oh, yeah. She'll be gone by the end of the month."

"Seriously?" I say, though it's more to myself than to him.

Andy, however, answers. "Yeah. I mean, I knew she was going to go travel again, but I figured she was going to wait to quit until December. What happened between you two? Is that why she's leaving now?"

Chloe and I haven't talked since she told me to fuck off. To be fair, I'm great at following directions and if you want me to fuck off, I will gladly do so. But seeing as I'm trying to put my life back together, Chloe leaving me alone and vaguely glaring at me from across the pub seems like the least of my worries.

"I don't know, Andy," I say and place the resignation letter back in the stack.

I hope not.

I sigh and head back out to the pub. In a way, I envy Chloe. Her ability to jump from one thing to the next and be so unafraid of quitting without having something else lined up. I've applied to a number of jobs, slightly related to singing and writing, but I refuse to quit until I have something to go to after. As much as I want to get the hell out of here and never come back, I can't yet. I need the reassurance that I'll have something to be productive with. Even if I don't feel very productive here.

I chat with some regulars sitting along the bar, drinking their usual beers or wines or whiskey on the rocks. I must admit that as much as I don't think this is my place, the pub has a great atmosphere. I understand why people come here every week. If I didn't work here, I might come for the food, the chats with the staff, the moody lighting, the indie music, the theme nights. Outside of this being a job, it's also a little slice of my peace.

I take a breath. How can you like a place and hate it at the same time?

"I guess there are positives and negatives to everything, right?"

I jump as a petite woman in front of me speaks and realize I asked that out loud.

"You think?" I say, recovering fast.

"Yeah, I feel like you can like what you've found

somewhere, maybe the community or something, but also have things you don't like about it." She pauses, studies me, and chews on her lip as she looks just to my left. "I assume you're talking about here, right? You've been people watching for the past little while."

I laugh. "I have been, haven't I?"

I let my eyes wander the pub again, but return my gaze to the woman's face. She seems to be around my age, with lily-white skin, short dark-brown hair, pixie-like features, and from what I can tell, a mermaid tattoo on her forearm. There's something in the furrow of her brow and her levelled gaze that makes me want to hear what she has to say.

"I hope you're not here next month."

My hand comes to my chest, mock offended. "Well, that's just rude."

"You've worked here for a while now, right? Forgive me for intruding or being weird or whatever; I know I can come off that way sometimes." She picks up a fry from the basket in front of her and I note the two small diamonds framing a pearl on her ring finger. "I just have the feeling that you're maybe not happy here. And maybe you don't think you deserve that? I don't know. Again, don't mind me if I'm wrong."

"You're not wrong," I say as she closes her eyes and rubs at her temple. She shakes her head. "Are you okay?"

"Yeah, just a headache." She pauses and glances down at my wrist. When her eyes meet mine again, they're lighter. "You should keep trying. Find what makes you happy again, Iris."

I pull my wrist back and cover it with my other hand. "Oh, no. I— That's my sister's bracelet. I don't know why I put it on today."

She shrugs as if this doesn't faze her, but her lips turn up in a satisfied smirk. "Usually when something like that happens, it's because we need a sign. I think you took Iris with you today."

My body runs cold and goosebumps form on my bare arms. I open my mouth to continue the conversation, ask her what the hell that meant and if Iris really is with me, but a man with deep brown skin and piercing green eyes appears by her side and kisses her cheek. She relaxes into him and smiles.

"Good to go, Clefairy?" he asks.

She laughs. "I don't know that one."

"It's pink," I say absently, then realize I'm now intruding on them. "I mean . . . The Pokémon, right?"

The man raises his eyebrows and grins at his fiancée. "See! Someone knows what I'm talking about."

"Congratulations." She giggles and slips her arms into the coat he holds out for her. She turns to me. "I hope you find what you're searching for."

She smiles at me warmly. He wraps an arm around her and leans close to her ear, as if whispering. I watch them make their way to the door, where she stops, turns back, and waves to me. I lift my hand and watch them go. My eyes stay trained on the door for some time. I reach forward absently to take away the now-empty basket of fries.

The chills remain. I don't know what it was about her, but something tells me I won't forget this moment for a long time.

"In a trance?"

For the second time tonight, I jump. This time, not because someone's speaking to me, but because of who it is. I look down at Chloe, crouched at the edge of the bar, picking up coins that have fallen from someone's wallet.

"You're talking to me again?" I ask.

"Well, yeah. I figure I should."

Chloe straightens and stands awkwardly in front of me, picking at stray threads on her apron. I've never seen her look so uncertain the whole time I've known her.

"Can we go somewhere and talk? We're not that busy. Take your break."

"I just got back from break."

She shrugs. "Give them a reason to fire you."

I don't even have time to laugh. She turns her back on me and walks toward the break room. I scan the pub. Andy, Zac, and two others are out and about. We're more than covered right now for the number of people here. I duck out before Andy notices me taking yet another break.

"Chloe," I say once I reach her.

She faces the whiteboard, doodling flames and a jet pack on a dick someone left there earlier today. I sigh and cross my arms over my chest and lean against the doorframe, waiting.

"Okay," she says, capping the red marker. "I don't owe you or anyone anything, but since I respect you and you're my friend . . . Here it is. I'm saying my piece and after that, that's it. No more talk about it for the next two weeks."

"What about after the next two weeks?" I ask.

She holds her ground and matches my pose, crossing her arms over her chest, tipping her chin up confidently.

"I'm leaving after that."

"For good?"

"It was a mistake coming back. I may have moved and work a town away from home, but it's not far enough. I don't know why I convinced myself I could start fresh when everyone I left is still right here. There's only so long you can avoid the past."

I sigh and push myself off the wall. I want to reach out to her, hold her hand or something like we used to do when there wasn't a weird distance in our friendship. "Why are you avoiding it?"

"Look, Magnolia, I was never meant to be a mom. I think I've known that my whole life, and I'm certain of it now. But I was eighteen when I got pregnant. I found out late, and I had this silly notion that it would make everything better in my life. I mean, Theo, you know Theo. He is such a great guy, and I think you know better than I do that he's a really great dad, too."

I nod when she pauses and take a few steps toward her. She deflates slightly as I wrap an arm around her shoulders.

"As I got closer and closer to giving birth, I just realized they would be better off without me. And I'm not saying that for sympathy or to be convinced otherwise. I'm not cut out for the mom life. Some people are and that's totally fine for them, but I'm not. Emma came early, before I'd really decided what I wanted to do. I probably could have made a better plan if I had time and maybe could have left without hurting Theo so badly, but I was young and stupid and hopped up on those hormones that happen after you give birth. I left two days later and never looked back, I guess, until now."

"How do you feel now?" I ask.

Chloe takes a shaky breath and swipes her hair away from her face. "I don't regret what I did. I just regret how I did it. When I found out you were dating Theo, I should have told you and talked to him, but I didn't. Instead, I avoided it and acted very childish. And then I lashed out at you because all my careful avoidance plans came crashing down. I'm sorry I fucked that up for you. You'd make a much better mom than I would."

"Chloe," I whisper, not entirely certain why my heart feels like it's breaking.

She smiles up at me. "It's true."

Silence settles between us as I digest her words. I don't know how she came to the decision that her little slice of family would be better off without her, but I respect her ability to make that choice. I understand why her parents cut contact with her after that. I understand why Theo carries anger from what happened. Above all, I think I understand her urge to run again.

"Chloe, I think you need to talk to Theo and your parents."

"Why?" she says with a scoff.

"Because explaining your side of things sometimes helps to mend fences. I'm not saying you have to jump into motherhood, but it might help all of you to . . . I don't know, grow? I think you all are still hurt from the situation. I know he is. I know you've struggled with your relationship with your parents, and I'm sure they're probably gutted to not have their only daughter in their lives anymore."

"Well, they have Emma," Chloe says and pushes away from me. She runs her hands absently along her apron. "Maybe you're right. I don't know. I guess I'll figure it out."

We stare at each other for a few beats of awkward silence. I shoot her a small, quick smile. She returns it, takes a breath, then leaves the room. I watch her retreating back and exhale.

Chapter Thirty-Six

The text comes in at 6:03 p.m. the following Friday. I miraculously have the day off from the pub, so naturally Mom feels comfortable asking for a favour.

Mom: I forgot half my kids' files at home. Will you drop them off for me?

Reluctantly, I agree because I need a walk, fresh air, and a break from my mind exploding as I try to write out my life plan. I've come up with a very unhelpful, but very definitive end goal of songwriter. And now I'm having an existential crisis, wondering if that could really be my life goal when I've already achieved that. I sold a song. My music and lyrics are out there in the world, so yes, I am a songwriter. But where the fuck do I go from there?

I find that walking does not help this. The cold is no help. All it does is make my cheeks feel like they're on fire and make me vaguely long for the winters where face masks kept the lower half of my face warm. As the white and rust brick of the one-hallway school appears in my sightline, I force my thoughts to stop. I refuse to let Mom know the depth of my freak-out. I'm out of distractions now and alone with my brain.

I cross the street and enter the packed parking lot. Every light inside the school is on, illuminating this patch of land much more than on a usual school night. My mom thrives on parent-teacher interviews. She somehow enjoys chatting with parents about their students, even though I feel like every other teacher on earth dreads this. But she loves talking about the good kids and loves calling out parents who aren't putting in the work. The duality of her personality.

I wonder what she might say to Theo.

The thought flickers through my mind and I physically stop in the middle of the parking lot. Wait. I step up on the curb and pull the file folder she'd asked for out of a random tote bag I'd picked up off the floor of my room. The blue folder is stuffed with papers. Pink, green, and blue sticky notes separate each group. At first glance, they look exactly like her student files. On closer inspection, they're dupes. Most of the pages are completely blank.

I close my eyes. "Come on."

I still haven't mentioned what's going on with Theo to either of my parents. Or Poppy, for that matter. But just like the first time I ran, Mom knows. I have no idea what she knows or what she thinks I can fix when he won't even talk to me, but just like at the ice rink, she's pulling for it. I sigh and consider leaving. I grab my phone out of my back pocket and absently dial her number. It goes to voicemail.

"Shit," I hiss.

Of course it would. She wouldn't be on her phone while she's in interviews. I turn and scan the parking lot for any familiar faces before I fully jump to conclusions and run home. All the cars in the lot look the same. Mostly minivans, with a small smattering of more upscale cars. Mostly black or silver, some red. I give up when I can't pinpoint Theo's car.

But I neglect to consider that he could have walked here just like I did.

"Magnolia?" I hear his voice behind me.

I turn and curse my mother. Curse the universe. Curse everyone who put this gorgeous man into my life just to pull him out and put him in front of me again looking so damn good in a pair of jeans and a seasonally questionable Henley.

"Where the hell is your coat?" I yell at him.

He shrugs, a sly little grin sneaking across his features. "I have a vest."

I bite back my own smile. My heart thuds wildly against my chest as he continues his approach. His body language is open, confident, casually swaggering towards me as if the past few weeks haven't happened. My brain shorts out at this, only forming the words *KISS. HIM. NOW.* in big neon letters. I shove the blue folder back into my bag and match his confident stroll. As I speed up, so does he. We crash together.

I don't let myself linger on the fact that both of our fights have ended in us kissing in a parking lot. I just kiss him.

His arms wrap around my waist and lift me from the ground for a moment. I smile against his lips, dotted with feverish kisses. My hands curl in his hair and glue his face to mine.

This. This is the kiss. This is the kiss that makes me want a life with him. This is the kiss that makes me want to tell him I love him. This is the kiss that makes me see into the future, sun blazing down on us as we walk down the aisle. This is the kiss that makes me feel so completely insane for thinking these things when it's only been two months, or maybe three, and we were only actually officially together for one of those months, but holy shit.

When you know, you know.

I get it now.

I pull back from him when I feel something wet hit my cheek. The first dusting of snowflakes falls softly around us. I tip my face up and stare at the sky, light grey bleeding into tones of pink.

"How's your vest?" I ask.

Theo removes one hand from my lower back and pulls something out of his pocket. "Good. I have a hat too."

I can't help the laugh that bubbles out of me. He pulls the beanie down over his ears and smirks. His hand cups my cheek and at first, I think he's going to kiss me again, but he just stares into my eyes. And, my God, I missed those eyes.

"What?" I whisper.

"I've missed you," he says.

I raise my eyebrows. "You're the one who stopped talking to me."

"I know," he says and drops his hand. He looks up at the sky, mournfully, blinking snow out of his eyes. "I just . . . I was so upset at you. At the world. Obviously, at Chloe. I just felt so blindsided, and I didn't want to talk. I desperately missed you and I wanted to tell you that, but I had been ignoring you. I felt really shitty about that, but even shittier about the fact that you knew her and didn't tell me."

"I genuinely had no idea who she was until that night."

"I know that now," he says and swallows. His Adam's apple bobs as he figures out his next words. "I mean, why would she tell people about that, you know? It makes sense that you wouldn't know and, when I thought back on it, you looked as blindsided as I felt."

I shake my head and feel as though I'm transported back to that parking lot. I was so convinced I'd lost everything with him right then and there.

"Why didn't you answer my texts and calls, then?"

"By the time I calmed down and thought rationally about that night, I thought I'd blown it. You'd stopped contacting me and I thought, fuck, that's it. I told you to try and I wasn't doing the same thing. I wasn't trying to see your side or get over my shit when I'd called you out." He laughs, shocking me, and sticks out a hand. "So, hello. My name's Theo, and I'm a hypocrite."

I take his hand. "You're in good company, then. I've been told I'm the same."

"You're not one."

"I am. I think we all are at one point or another, but I'm trying not to be."

Theo nods. A set of parents walk from the school and Theo pulls me to the side and unintentionally into a wall so they can pass. I giggle as he collides with me, feeling like a teenager sneaking around school, finding a little alcove to make out with her boyfriend.

"What're you doing?" he asks. He holds me close against his body, his lips inches from mine. "You don't have to tell me. I realize I pushed your old plan on you without fully hearing you out, and I'm sorry for that. I understand if you don't want to talk about it because of that, but I am interested in knowing about your life."

"I don't know yet," I say after a moment and drop my gaze to his shoes. He snakes a finger along my jawline, ending at my chin to tip my face back up to his. "I'm trying to figure out what I want from life now that Iris is gone. I'm trying to sort out what she wanted versus what I want. I don't know if they're the same thing."

He brushes a hair away from my face and smiles. I still haven't figured out how to style much shorter hair, but a hat seems to do the trick for the most part.

"You know it's okay if it's not the same, right?"

I nod, tears forming in my eyes. "I do. On some level, I guess. I talked to her after you left the pub. I went to her grave for the first time since she died because I felt like I was losing everything, including her and my grasp on myself . . . I feel guilty moving on without her, like I'm not supposed to choose something she doesn't want because that was the plan. But I don't know if I want the plan."

"Well, you know how my plans worked out," Theo says with a laugh. This time, though, his laugh comes out miles less bitter than it used to. He takes a deep breath. "Sometimes plans change, and that's okay. Chloe actually came and talked to me. Brought Emma a birthday present. And though I don't think I'll ever be fully okay with what she did, I'm learning how to let go of that anger."

I wasn't sure if Chloe was ever going to take my advice, but it means a lot. I sigh and press a quick kiss to Theo's lips. "I'm happy for you. I wish I could let go as well."

"You will, someday."

"What if I never figure it out?"

"You will. I know you will. So you're floundering because things didn't go to plan. So what? Sometimes life throws all your plans out the window and makes you deal with it, and that sucks. That rock bottom feeling is the worst. But it doesn't last. Eventually you get to a point where the thing you wanted isn't what you wanted anymore and what you have now is better." His eyes flash, pupils expanding as they bore into mine. His thumb caresses my cheek. "And you don't have to have another plan. You can figure it out as you go. You can try and enjoy the process."

"That sounds incredibly not enjoyable."

He laughs. "I'm not going to lie, sometimes it's not. But sometimes . . ."

Sometimes your boyfriend pushes you against a wall and kisses you senseless. I can no longer feel my fingers, and my knees are weak. I don't know if it's from the cold or from him. Theo exudes warmth, somehow. I grip his biceps and feel the heat radiating beneath. I have no clue how he's still warm in this weather, in his vest, but his warmth fills me up. My whole body burns, and I desperately wish we were both inside and at home so that I could peel away his clothes and run my hands along his sculpted chest. His mouth moves hungrily against mine and my breath comes out in frantic bursts.

He hooks his fingers into the loops of my jeans and pulls me closer to him. I don't care that the snow is falling harder around us. I don't care that anyone could walk out and see what we're doing. I desperately need this *sometimes* moment. Because his lips feel like the first snowfall before Christmas or the first rain in the middle of a drought. And truly, what is better than the hypnotic, toe-curling, mind-melting moment when your lover calms your stormy thoughts and creates a whole other storm of emotions coursing through your body?

This moment brings me the absolute certainty that I would let him burn my body down over and over again, for the rest of my life.

I only pull away from him when my phone rings.

"Hello?" I answer, slightly breathless.

"Magnolia!" Mom says, too enthusiastic on the other end of the phone. Theo chuckles when he hears her voice come through. "I was just checking up on you."

"I'm fine!"

"Did you get my files?"

"Did I get . . . Oh!" I glance down at the snow-dusted garden bed where my tote bag has fallen, then smile up at Theo. His arms tighten around my waist. "Yeah, I got them."

Chapter Thirty-Seven

I return home to the exact same place I'd left over an hour ago: my bed. My body is a mixture of freezing cold from being outside all that time and pleasantly warm from being in Theo's arms. My mind, however momentarily soothed, still travels in rather confusing patterns. It feels as though the ceiling is spiralling the more I stare up at it. I cover my eyes with my hands and press my palms against them.

At a creak from my door, I sit up, pooling my sheets around me. Dad walks in, shirt sleeves still bunched at the elbows and slightly wet from giving Poppy a bath. She's asleep now, snuggled up in her crib with Iris's old bear. Dad sits on the edge of my bed and faces the door he just walked through. He takes off his glasses and rubs at his eyes, then leaves the glasses resting on his knee.

"Dad?" I whisper.

An uneasy silence forms between us. I don't know how to break it, so I sit there and wait for him to speak, fear balling itself up in the pit of my stomach because I remember what happened the last time he came and sat on my bed at a loss for words, not quite knowing what to say. Iris was dead.

"Magnolia, you know I'm proud of you, right?" he finally says.

"I— Yes," I say and untangle myself from my sheets. I scramble to sit next to him. I stare at the side of his face until he looks at me. Pain colours his eyes. Deep lines of concern trace themselves across his forehead. "What's going on?"

"I feel like I've failed you." He sighs deeply.

"You're joking, right?" I say and can't help the incredulous laugh that comes along with it. "How would you ever come to that conclusion?"

He shakes his head. "I want to be honest with you. I think it's something you deserve after the past two years. I know how it seemed when you got back from your trip. You came back home, and we'd cleaned out Iris's old room to make space for Poppy. Your mom and I were just going about life like nothing was wrong. Your mom went back to work after you agreed to take care of Poppy, though I know you felt you didn't have much of a choice. We still laughed and danced and watched our silly romance movies. It looked like everything was just business as usual. I know you suffered from our pretence."

"Pretence?" I say slowly and train my gaze on the free-standing rack of clothing next to my bed that fits everything that won't go in my closet. I blink away newly formed tears. "I don't follow. What were you pretending?"

"I don't know how much you remember directly after Iris died," he says and takes a shuddering breath, as if saying his eldest daughter's name out loud is a challenge. "We all took that hit hard. As we should have. You don't— When something like that happens, it just— There are no words for the grief you feel when someone dies before their time should have been up. When it's your child—" His voice breaks and he doesn't continue the statement. I impulsively reach out and grab hold of his hand. "Iris's death broke your mother. I watched her break into pieces every day. I think you were too entrenched in your own grief to notice that. But I watched the two of you through my own desolation and felt so helpless."

"I'm so sorry," I whisper. "I remember shutting down and just not talking to you guys. And then I left."

"You did." He squeezes my hand and smiles at me sadly. "You did what you had to do. Don't apologize. But you were gone, and you didn't see how desperately your mom and I tried to rebuild our lives from there. We struggled, but we eventually found a rhythm that worked for us. Unfortunately, you didn't get to see that. You started to heal in your own way, then got dropped into unfamiliar territory. We should have worked harder to bring you into that, to see how you wanted to move forward as well."

I swallow the lump in my throat, but my voice still manages to come out as a rasp. "You guys never talk about her."

"I know," he whispers. "It worked for a while. It helped your mom to not mention every single little thing that reminded us of her. We did that a lot at first and it always broke us down. We cried so many tears over the little memories. It worked better to pretend for a while."

"Like she didn't exist?"

The question sits in the silence of my room. The room that Iris and I decorated together. The one place where she still feels semi-alive. I stare at my dad's profile, crumbled in sadness and shame. He closes his eyes, allowing tears to flow in rivulets down his face, and nods slowly.

"I never pretended she didn't exist, but sometimes . . . Sometimes it felt better to forget for a moment. Sometimes I pretend she's still alive, and that way I don't have to remember all the little things. I don't have to say or think her name every day because she's still alive. But sometimes that pretending hurts more than not talking about her."

"When's the last time you talked about her?" I ask. He doesn't answer and I take that to mean this is the first time in a long while, apart from the briefest mention after I dyed my hair. "Maybe we should all sit down and have an Iris day. We could go to a play that she liked or, I don't know, just do something to intentionally remind us that she lived." I sniff and consider my next words, whether they'll help or hinder. I play with the delicate gold bracelet that bears her name around my wrist. I've worn it every day for a week. "I always feel so much lighter when I talk about her. Whenever I let her back into my life, it feels right. Maybe it didn't at first, but it does now. Theo was the first one to get me to talk about her because I hadn't at all since her death. Maybe we needed outside perspective."

"Maybe," Dad says. He blinks away more tears as he meets my eyes. "This is why I feel I've failed you, Bug."

I shake my head, too overcome by emotion to tell him just how wrong he is. My tears finally fall as well, and I let Dad gather me in his lap.

"I know how long you've struggled. I've seen you trying to get back on your feet and I've never figured out how to help you back up. And, God, I'm trying now, but I still don't know what you need. How can I help you? What do you need?"

"I don't know. I think I want to talk about Iris, though. I kind of want to bring her back into the house. Can we put her pictures up again? Have you talked to Mom?"

"Not yet. But I will. We have to support each other better moving forward, and I think it's officially time we moved into the next circle of hell."

I laugh through a sob and wipe a hand over my eyes. Dad catches my wrist and stares down at Iris's bracelet. He smiles.

Chapter Thirty-Eight

"So I may have done something stupid and impulsive, and I still don't quite know how I feel about it," I say to Theo as I approach him in the school parking lot, Poppy balanced on my hip.

He straightens off the hood of his car and eyes me warily. I smile in return as Poppy squirms, desperately trying to claw her way over to Theo. I laugh as she somehow maneuvers herself away from me and magically appears in his arms.

"What did you do?" he asks, glancing at me briefly while still entertaining Poppy. She babbles to him in a mix of English and Poppy-speak. He nods as if he understands every word, and maybe, like me, he does.

Theo and I lapsed back into our relationship easily. We talked things out over coffee and hot chocolate while Rocket sat on my feet, as if telling me I was stuck with them now. Truthfully, I didn't have a problem with that. Theo laid out some ground rules so Emma wouldn't get hurt, and I happily agreed. Together we decided we have to communicate with each other, even when it gets hard, instead of getting upset and running. We shook on it, then sealed it with a kiss. Then a little bit more than a kiss.

"Before I tell you what I did, Miss Poppy here would like to invite you to her birthday party."

Poppy hands him the envelope she's been clutching between her fingers since we walked out the door. I hesitated to give it to her, but she cried until I gave in, then treated it like it was her baby. Theo takes the envelope and grins.

"I would love to come to your party!" he announces. Poppy claps, then throws herself at him for a hug. He eyes me above her head. "What did you do?"

"I finally emailed the head of the program back and she invited me to the showcase so we could chat."

"Are you going to go?" Theo asks. He tries hard to suppress his excitement from my words, but I can see it blooming in him just behind his eyes.

"Will you come with me?"

Poppy adamantly wanted a dog-themed birthday party. I scrambled around for days finding dog-shaped balloons, paw print plates, and the perfect cake topper. Mom offered to help, but I took the full reins. I'd say it's worth it now, even if I did just plan the whole thing to keep my mind off the impending Holiday Showcase.

I smile as Poppy wanders around from person to person in her puppy dog ears. She thrives on the attention, making sure everyone gets a hug and a scrunch-nosed smile. Her flowery dress fluffs out around her, making her look like a woodland princess.

Theo sidles up to me and hands me a cup filled with nacho chips. I snicker my thanks and crunch a chip. His hand finds my hipbone as I lean against him.

"You doing all right?" he whispers below conversations swirling around us.

Because it's Theo, he's been sensitive to how we might be feeling and has made sure to ask how we're all doing the past few days. Try as we might, and as happy as we are to see Poppy grow, this week in December holds bad memories.

"I'm okay, I think," I say. I give him a small smile. "Sad, but I guess that's expected. Poppy helps, though. She's cute enough that I don't really feel the sadness too much."

"Okay, good. I was going to suggest smashing some cake in your face if you weren't."

I scoff. "I would enjoy that more if I could do that to you."

"Of course you would."

"You offered."

Poppy skips over to me and Theo, Emma holding her hand. Every child at the party got their own headband. Emma's dog-ear headband is the same as Poppy's, taupe brown with flowers between the ears. Poppy made sure.

"Looking good, dawgs," Theo says, making me and Emma roll our eyes. Apparently, the Dad Joke gene is innate in all men.

"Poppy was asking me about cake," Emma says, eyes wide and innocent.

While I believe that Poppy probably did ask about cake, I'm confident that Emma didn't need her arm twisted to ask as well. Which is totally fair because I did make a pretty damn good cake, if I do say so myself.

I sigh and scan the group for my mom. The house is mostly filled with extended family. Cousins who have their own kids now being the main guests because Mom wanted Poppy to have people to play with. A few of my mom's teaching friends are here as well, plus neighbours we've grown close to over the years, and Hanna, who had to leave early for work.

"I'll see what I can do," I say to Emma once I find my mom.

I brush past the three of them and take myself and my nacho cup into the kitchen. Mom pulls more cheese blocks out of the fridge and sets them on the mostly demolished cheese tray. She turns to me with a grin that probably only I can tell is forced.

"Hey!" I say and pinch a piece of mozzarella cheese off the new pile. "Pops was wondering about cake."

"She's been thinking about cake all day," Mom says, as if this is a bad thing.

"And so have I," I say with a smirk. "Theo's offered to be the one to get it smashed in his face, if you're down for that."

"Save that for your wedding," she quips and, to my surprise, pulls out dessert plates. I raise my eyebrows. "What? It's time for dessert. We've had our main meal."

She walks past me before I have a chance to respond. I cock my head and follow her with my eyes as she reaches the cake table. Well, that was easy. Poppy zeroes in on Mom and books it toward her cake. I cringe when I remember that Poppy is wearing tights and has never been good at putting on the breaks. I have visions of the cake table crashing to the ground and making a much more elaborate mess than if Theo or I smashed the cake in each other's faces.

But not for the first time, Theo's dad reflexes kick in and he manages to grab Poppy before she falls face first into icing. She grins up at him and sticks her fingers into the cake anyway. I crack up, laugh echoing from my spot in the kitchen.

I rush over to Poppy and Theo, thankful that my mom somehow hasn't noticed the commotion in her preoccupation with plates, utensils, and candles. Theo grabs a fistful of napkins to remove the icing glued to Poppy's fingers, while I reach for the cake. I painstakingly piped little blush-coloured rosettes on every inch of the cake last night, then, this morning, added the topper I ordered from Etsy. I pluck the Dalmatian sitting on top of a large pink dog bone bearing Poppy's name out of the rosettes, rotate the cake 180 degrees, and push it back in. Theo shoots me a thumbs-up, dirty napkins stuffed in the front pocket of his jeans.

"All right, everyone!" Mom says, sticking a number two candle into the cake. Her brows furrow when she notices the blemished icing I turned to the back. "It's time to wish a certain someone a happy birthday!"

Dad appears at my side, his poppy tie around his neck specially for today, and pulls a chair over to the dessert table. He lifts Poppy onto the chair and miraculously manages to hold her back from the cake. I step to the side, finding Theo once more, and pull out my phone. I begin filming as the group sings to Poppy rather off tune, but full to the brim with love for this little creature.

I blink away the tears that come to my eyes when the duality of singing "Happy Birthday" to Poppy just mere days before the anniversary of Iris's death hits me. A moment later, I nearly laugh at the most absurd thought. Why do we never sing "Happy Death Day" on the day that someone died? Theo catches my unhinged look and narrows his eyes. His hand finds my waist and tangles in the ruched fabric of my floral dress.

"I'll tell you later," I whisper to him as the crush of voices finish the birthday song.

Poppy leans toward the cake and meets my dad's eyes as he tries to tell her how to blow out a candle. Instead, she drools down her chin and giggles. Dad leans in with her and pretends she blew it out with a breath of her own. He kisses her cheek, and she hugs his face.

I don't notice the tear that slips from my eye until Theo wipes it away. I smile at him because I'm not sad, really. I'm just so glad that even though this little human had to lose the most important person to her, she's still so incredibly loved.

Chapter Thirty-Nine

I'm not sure what form of serendipity dictates that the Holiday Showcase falls on the anniversary of Iris's death, but it's definitely something. This fact stalled me when I first read the email. My thoughts halted and I actually considered responding with a resounding *no* just at the sheer chance of it. But Theo thought maybe it meant something. Maybe it was a sign from Iris that I was going in the right direction.

Theo reaches across the centre console of his car and grabs hold of my hand. He squeezes it gently. I shakily sigh and stare impassively at the snow falling past the windshield. The snow barrels down so fast, illuminated by headlights just after sunset, that it feels as though we're flying through space, past streaky galaxies and stars. My nerves are on edge. I'm unbalanced and anxious and feel an acute sense of grief gnawing in the pit of my stomach.

"It's going to be okay," Theo says, his eyes straying momentarily from the road to meet mine. "No matter what happens tonight, no matter what you or the head of the program decides, it's going to be okay."

"How can you be so sure?" I whisper. "When nothing's

been okay for the past two years . . . How do you know it suddenly will be now?"

"Because you have the power to make it be okay. You can change your life, if you want, or you can carry on along the same path."

I close my eyes. I admire his ability to think so positively of me and just in general. Maybe I admire it so much because that used to be me. And outside of it being the day when my grief over Iris's death hangs so crushingly on my shoulders, I still haven't reached a spot where I do think positively about my future.

"Besides," Theo says, and I open my eyes, sensing he's about to shoot the shit. "You have me, so you're doubly okay."

I roll my eyes and slap his shoulder jokingly. I settle back into my seat, then smile and squeeze his hand. Maybe I can do this.

But my doubts creep back in as we pull off the Gardiner Expressway. I close my eyes again and let myself be jostled by the gentle movement of the car. We travel down slushy streets in stop-and-go traffic, drivers careful or careless in the ongoing snow. Theo nudges me.

"Look," he says as we slowly pass by the old stone buildings of the University of Toronto's downtown campus. "That's where I went to school for a year. And then I stupidly transferred to Scarborough campus because the commute in here clearly wasn't far enough."

I giggle, which dissipates some of the tension eating at me. Theo recalls first-year anecdotes and distracts me from the fact that Koerner Hall is fast approaching. He points out the ROM and I crinkle my nose, as if I haven't been there a million times like any good Canadian girl growing up in the GTA. He enthusiastically talks about his adventures at the McDonald's near campus, kiddy corner from the ROM. I laugh at the French fry bet he and his friend made early on in his first year that resulted in several large fries being decimated and only a little bit of vomit. I avert my eyes from the concert hall hosting the Royal Conservatory of Music's showcase performance tonight.

Theo miraculously finds a parking garage with tons of parking off Bloor. He pulls into a spot and kills the engine.

"Are you ready to go?" he asks. I shake my head. "Are you as ready as you'll be?"

I laugh and surprise myself at the catch in my throat. "Yeah, I guess I am. I don't see myself getting more ready. Do I— How do I look?"

"You look perfect. I would take you back."

"I don't know how reliable that is coming from someone who already took me back."

"Touché," he says, then drums his fingers on the steering wheel. "Maybe that makes me more reliable."

I grimace and pull the door handle. Snow blows through the slatted partitions of the parking garage. I let the wind blow my hair around my face. I inhale deeply. Theo comes around to my side of the car and places his hand on the small of my back. I can feel his heat through the fabric of my peacoat and satin red dress. I lean into him as we walk toward the theatre.

We pass the Varsity Blues billboard outside of Varsity Stadium, all domed up for the winter. Koerner Hall sits next to it in all its glory. I've been here before. Many times, for many different performances, whether for school functions or other Royal Conservatory events. I've stood under the glass front of the building, right next to the castle-like mansion that houses the Royal Conservatory of Music, then walked inside and marvelled at the expansive wooden theatre that houses up to a thousand people and that gorgeous stage. That stage that fills you with such awe whether you're on it or in the audience.

I take a deep breath of cold, fresh air. Theo's hand tightens against me. He smiles and nudges me forward.

"You're okay," he whispers. His hand rubs my back soothingly. "Or you will be okay. But if you don't want to do this, you don't have to."

"No, I want to," I say, and we walk inside the concert hall.

I remember this atmosphere. Everyone talks to each other excitedly, making it hard to hear yourself think, overall amping up every single person in this space. Theo guides me through the crowds, intuitively sensing I'm not capable of interaction today. He walks us through the lobby and into the auditorium. The last time I was here was two days before Iris gave birth. Everything's changed since then.

Theo reads the numbers and letters on seats to himself as I absently trail behind him. Our seats are near the front, Arielle made sure. She always sits first row, centre. I'm sure she gave us these seats so she could see immediately whether I'd shown up or not. I avert my eyes and stare at the ground, not quite ready to talk. Theo gestures to a chair and I lower myself into it, sinking into the black cushion.

"How you doing?" he asks after he's shrugged out of his coat and settled in his chair. I keep mine on, too afraid to let any warmth leave my body.

"Weird. I'm doing weird," I say. I scan the room, quickly filling up. It's nearly showtime. "It's been a bit since I've been here."

"Yeah, I was thinking about that. You probably haven't been here since . . . she died."

"And now I'm here exactly two years later." I swallow the rush of emotion. "Odds I cry tonight?"

"I wouldn't bet against it," he quips. He finds my hand again and loops our fingers. "But I don't think that's a bad thing."

"No, maybe not," I say as the lights go down.

I hold my breath when Arielle appears on stage. The audience erupts in applause. She looks exactly as she did before. All elegance and grace. Her glossy black hair cascades down her back, wide eyes highlighted by clear-rimmed glasses shine with excitement and pride, hands clasped in front of her with a ring on each finger. Everything may have changed, but some things never do. Theo squeezes my hand.

"Good evening, everyone! Thank you all for coming out on such a blustery night!"

I zone out for the rest of her speech, hearing everything but not fully digesting it. I go to a place in the recesses of my mind where all my brain cells that require thinking and feeling are on vacation and protect myself from everything I missed out on. I stare off into the distance and intentionally think of absolutely nothing.

And then the first person steps out on stage.

The room explodes in colour. My heart thumps against my chest. My stomach unclenches and if it were possible, butterflies would fly right out of me. Without warning, tears leak from my eyes, and I find myself smiling. Theo's arm wraps around me. I grin into his side, my attention rapt on the current singer.

I stay that way for nearly two hours, switching between laughter and tears. I slip out of my coat as my soul reignites. My smile unwavering.

When the show ends, I'm one of the first people on my feet. Forgetting that Theo's hand is firmly placed in mine, I yank him up along with me. He laughs at my delight and in a wacky, probably dopamine-filled haze, I kiss him. He loops an arm around me and matches the brief but furious movement of my lips. I pull back and cheer as the showcase performers take their bows. I haven't felt this elated since I got off the stage at that karaoke restaurant with Theo, and before that, I hadn't felt this since I was on this very stage.

"How're you feeling now?" Theo asks, caught up in the excitement swirling around us.

I laugh. "Good. I'm feeling good!"

I spot Arielle back in her seat at the front of the theatre and know what I have to do. As if sensing someone boring a hole in the back of her head, she turns and glances at me. I wave and, to my surprise, she meanders her way through the aisles and saunters up to me and Theo.

"Magnolia!" she says and opens her arms, inviting me into a hug. "It's so nice to see you again."

"It's so great to be back here," I say into her ear.

She pulls back and takes a good look at me. I self-consciously push a short wave of hair behind my ear and fold my arms over my chest. Theo rubs my hip, subtle enough that only I can feel it. I drop my hand and land on top of his. Arielle smiles.

"And who is this?" she asks.

I tip my face up to Theo, a slow smile spreading across my lips. "This is my boyfriend, Theo."

They both stick out their hands at the same time. "Pleasure to meet you."

"Likewise," Theo says. "This was such an amazing show you put on."

"One of the best, I think," Arielle says, then turns her attention back to me. Her eyes, creased with laugh lines and wisdom from her innumerable years in music, meet mine. I keep her gaze. "Now, Magnolia, I'm not going to make you beg or anything, but I'd like to hear why you'd like back into the program."

"I don't," I say, surprising myself at the forwardness, but not surprised at the ease with which it comes out. Theo's grip loosens on me, and I can feel his inquisitive eyes on my skull. Arielle, on the other hand, looks pleased.

"Good. Much as I loved having you here, dear, I never thought it was what you wanted. You are too good for my program."

I laugh, a little self-conscious, and hide my face. "I remember in my second year you asked me why I was here, and I didn't have an answer. I've never had my own answer for why I wanted to be a singer or why I was pursuing this. I think it took Iris's death for me to realize that it wasn't my dream. It was hers. And as much as I love performing, my passion has always been in writing music and lyrics."

"I recognized that in you. It's why I always offered the more creative options to you. It's rare that students sing their own songs during the showcase, but you were going to do that."

"I was. In a way, I wish I got the chance to sing it."

"Perhaps you will, someday. Maybe here, maybe not. All I know is that you never needed me to get you where you want to go. Where are you going now?"

I flush and stare down at the floor. I take a breath and decide I'm done being coy about it. I'm going to own it just like I did the first time I sold a song. I meet Arielle's eyes again and from the smirk on her lips, I can tell the fire in me is palpable.

"I've been writing songs again. They're mostly love songs," I say with a laugh and a quick glance at Theo. He winks back at me. "But a lot of them are also about death and grieving. I didn't write for a long time after Iris died, and that may have been part of my problem. I started up again recently and the words didn't stop. I have a lot to put out into the world. And I know the process is long and daunting before you get a name of your own, especially when you haven't put anything out since you were nineteen . . . So I've also applied for a few music-related jobs. Session singers and music teachers, mostly."

She claps her hands together and grins. "Excellent! When you get home tonight, send me an email. I might know of an opening for you that would allow you enough space to work on your own personal projects."

"You're serious?"

"Of course," she says and touches my upper arm. "You're looking for an agent as well? I might know someone. You are destined for great things. It starts here. Today."

Chapter Forty

Theo and I celebrated my breakthrough in the car in that parking garage with ravenous, hungry hands, then got McDonald's at his old haunt. We stayed out late, driving, talking about the jobs I'd applied for, my newfound excitement for the future, and Arielle's offer.

I walk through the front door just after two in the morning. The lights are on in the kitchen and my brow furrows as I take this in. Normally, my parents would be asleep by now. But as a rush of air leaves my chest, I realize for the first time since leaving Koerner Hall that today is not a normal day.

"Mom?" I call out after removing my winter clothes and shuffling my way into the kitchen.

She doesn't answer at first, her back to me. Goosebumps form on my bare arms. I can't tell what she's doing from this angle, exactly, but her hands are busy with something on the wall. Her short golden hair is pulled back in a tiny sprout of a ponytail, held with a green scrunchie that perfectly matches her plaid Christmas pyjamas. I watch her shoulders rise and fall.

"Yes, Lia?" Mom says, her voice breaking slightly.

She turns to me, giving me a fuller picture of the wall behind her. I subconsciously take a few steps closer. Next to my high school graduation photo on the wall, a relic that's been there for seven years now, is Iris's university graduation photo. My breath catches. This photo came down while I was travelling. It was the first evidence of her I noticed was gone when I got back home. Mom's eyes follow my gaze, and she gives me a wan smile.

"Come. Sit," she says and pulls out a chair for me.

I slide onto the chair and curl my body into itself, drawing my knees to my chest, nearly slipping off the seat in my satin dress. Mom walks to the counter and pours from the translucent kettle that sits next to the toaster. She places two mugs of steeping tea on the table, followed by a bowl of sugar and a saucer of milk. I reach for the milk and pour some into my tea until it turns a pale shade of brown. When I look up, Mom is staring at me.

"What?" I ask.

"How was your night?" Mom asks, leaning forward to take a sip of her tea.

Out of everything, I wasn't expecting her to say that, so I just blink at her impassively for a moment. "I'm sure you can tell from my face. My makeup didn't stay." I laugh, lightly. "It was good. Cathartic. It let me fully admit what I wanted."

"And what's that?"

"I know you might not like it, but I want to be a songwriter. And maybe I'll even indulge you and be a music teacher while I get myself there. But I want to have that feeling of hearing my song and feeling good about myself again. The past few years, every time I heard it, I felt . . . shame, I think. Can you believe that?"

Mom nods. "I can. I think it's the same thing I've felt walking into this house the past two years."

"Oh, Mom," I say as she swipes a hand across her also makeup-less eyes.

"Everything comes back to Iris, doesn't it? I've tried my damnedest to ignore the fact that everything is a memory, but I'm learning that's not the right way to go."

My eyes shift to the photo to my right. Our home used to be a shrine to the two of us. There were photographs of me and Iris everywhere, but slowly hers disappeared, replaced by ones of Poppy. I stare into Iris's dark eyes, bright and exuberant. I remember her elation on the day she graduated. She was so confident that one day she would be my manager, and I was too taken by her enthusiasm to tell her that wasn't what I wanted.

"I haven't heard you say her name in ages," I say, barely above a whisper. I stare at Iris's megawatt smile until my eyes blur and I can't keep the tears at bay.

"What a fool I've been," Mom says.

Her eyes are trained on the photo as well, tears streaming down her face. I reach out and grab her hand across the table. She entwines our fingers and squeezes, hard.

"You're not a fool. You've just been trying to live like the rest of us."

Her lips quirk up briefly. "That's what I've been trying to do for two years. I've carried on, living as normal for you and Poppy. I didn't realize how much that would hurt."

"I don't think it's ever going to be painless," I say. I stare into the bubbles forming on top of my tea. "I think it hurts more to forget, though. I've felt as though I was in a kind of limbo, where everything reminded me of her, but no one wanted to talk about it. I tried to do the forgetting thing, but I think it hurt me more in the long run. It got me stuck."

"I know what you mean," Mom says with a deep sigh. "I thought I was doing the right thing and managing . . . Your dad and I had a talk a few days ago. Seems we've all been feeling a bit stuck lately. Something definitely needs to change in how we've dealt with Iris's death."

I nod and bite my lip. "I just keep thinking that Poppy's going to ask about her one day, and maybe it'd be easier for her if Iris was actually a part of our lives instead of something we tried to hide."

Mom stifles a sob. She closes her eyes and lets the tears fall. I place my left hand on top of our clasped hands. Just like Dad, Mom glances down and notices my wrist with Iris's delicate chain bracelet. Mom brings her other hand down and runs her fingers along the name. She shakes her head.

"How did I get so lucky to have such a lovely daughter like you?" she asks.

I shrug, my cheeks heating. "You got lucky with both of us. And Poppy. The worst of your luck was the day Iris died, but we were so lucky just to know her."

"We were. We really were."

Chapter Forty-One

One week later, I'm back at The Ranch. Poppy clings to me, desperately trying to steal all the warmth from my body. The barn isn't outright cold, but it has wooden walls and no heater, so yeah, she's unhappy. I try to lure her away from my body with a donut.

"Pops, come on," I say, walking toward the elaborate food table set up along the back wall. "You know you want a donut!"

Of course she refuses, so I move to a free spot just by the entryway to the stalls and lean against a wooden beam. I take a large bite of the classic glazed Krispy Kreme donut and suppress a groan from it being the first thing I've eaten this morning.

It's the end-of-year Christmas party for all the horse girls. Emma, eager to show me she had gotten back on the horse, told me I should come. Theo agreed and I walked right back into the place they left for me in their lives. We all piled into Theo's car and made the trek out on a thankfully sunny, but chilly, day. The party is in the barn, decked out with garlands and a clearly last-minute, haphazardly decorated Christmas tree in one corner. The girls mingle with each other and the horses in their stalls, while the adults generally huddle around a hot-chocolate-making station, basically the only source of warmth in here. I've found that the archways into different sections of the barn also somehow seem a bit warmer than elsewhere, so here I am.

Theo pulls me to his chest and Poppy slinks into his arms. He exudes heat, regardless of how freezing it is outside.

"You get used to it," Theo says. "I've stood in this barn for so many hours just watching lessons."

I smile, glad that Emma decided to go back after getting her cast off.

"Not that it would matter to you," I say with an eyebrow raise. "I bet you showed up in shorts last week, you freak."

His already red-from-the-cold cheeks flush further. He nudges me teasingly, then kisses the top of my head. I relax into him and close my eyes. His free arm comes around me and rests on my hip while Poppy buries her face in his warm neck. I can't hold back the smile on my face. Our bodies fit so perfectly together, even through layers of winter wear and puffy coats.

"This is the happiest I've felt in a long time," I mumble.

Theo's grip tightens around me, pulling me ever so slightly closer to him. "I'm so proud of you. Everything's coming together. There's no one more deserving."

I'm thankful he can't see my face in our current position. My cheeks flame and once more, my grin is impossible to hold back. I quit my job at the pub the day after the showcase. I knew I wasn't going to immediately find employment, but if I didn't quit, I knew I'd never have the courage to try. With shaking hands, I sent Arielle an email, then called her when she requested. She couldn't offer me much right now, but she wanted me. So she forwarded me along to someone higher up, who then offered me a job playing piano in the lobby of various buildings belonging to the Royal Conservatory of Music. I had to audition for it, but it all felt so natural. I'd forgotten the joy of making music for other people.

I already know this isn't my permanent landing place, but it is a place to land for now. It's a steppingstone amongst steps I actually want to take now. Steps I finally feel able to take. I start in January, and I honestly could not be more excited. Arielle also told an agent about me. It's no guarantee, and I haven't heard back from him yet, but it feels like something's moving, or at least it's giving me a little bit of a confidence boost.

"Happy Christmas Eve Eve," Theo says.

I laugh at the *Friends* reference and turn my face to him. His eyes are warm and bright, and slightly watery from the cold, making them look like crystals. I place a hand on his cheek and point above us. His gaze follows my finger to the plant tied together with a bright-red ribbon.

"Mistletoe," I say.

His eyes come back to mine and a slow, sly smile spreads across his lips. "Do you think I need an excuse to kiss you?"

"What're you waiting for?" I ask.

Theo leans in and our lips meet. His hand snakes just beneath my puffer jacket, thumb brushing the gap of skin between my jeans and cardigan. We're well aware that we're in public and around children, so it's short and sweet, but I feel the kiss in my bones. I pull back at Poppy's insistence, a hand coming between our faces. She playfully smacks both of us and waves a finger around.

"No!" Poppy says. "No!"

Theo and I burst into laughter and Poppy's face softens. She gives us a crinkle-nosed smile before sticking her nose right back on Theo.

"God, I love her," I muse and pat her spunky little back. I hear a giggle muffled against Theo's neck.

Theo tilts his head toward me and catches my chin with a finger. I lick my lips and taste the hot chocolate leftover from his kiss.

"I love you," Theo says.

I place my hand flat against his chest, feeling his heart beating steadily beneath it. His fingers absently play with a curl of hair by my ear.

"No fair," I whisper, looping a finger through a gap in his flannel button-up. "I was going to say it first."

Theo grins. "Beat you to it."

"Rude," I breathe against his lips. "I love you too, Theo Hennessy."

And just like we both deserve, we get our great, cinematic, earth-shattering kiss. Poppy doesn't interrupt this time, just giggles as her apple friend metaphorically sweeps me off my feet and lets me know that I am home.

Emergency Lullabies: The Playlist

1. right where you left me | Taylor Swift
2. A Safe Place to Land | Sara Bareilles feat. John Legend
3. Visiting Hours | Ed Sheeran
4. If I Die Young | The Band Perry
5. Good To You | Marianas Trench
6. Apple Pie | Lizzy McAlpine
7. Time Alive | KC Katalbas
8. Where Would I Be | Lady A
9. Toronto | Jon Robert Hall
10. Thank You For The Music | Amanda Seyfried
11. You Belong | Rachel Platten
12. I Was Made For Loving You | Tori Kelly feat. Ed Sheeran
13. I'm Fine | Ashe
14. 24 | sundial
15. Why Am I Like This? | Orla Garland
16. You Are In Love | Taylor Swift
17. You Matter To Me | Drew Gehling, Jessie Mueller
18. I Get To Love You | Ruelle
19. I Love You | Alex and Sierra
20. Feel Alive | Katie Herzig
21. First Aid Kit | Maddie Poppe
22. Late Night Talking | Harry Styles
23. Line By Line | JP Saxe feat. Maren Morris
24. Iris | Kina Grannis

Acknowledgements

I wrote Emergency Lullabies in November and December of 2021, before I'd experienced any big grief in my life. It was inspired by a simple interaction I saw at a splash park that August. When I returned to this book several months later, my grandmother had passed away and my family had gone through the period of adjustment that happens after a loss. I'd like to think that knowing how crushing, yet hopeful, yet sad, yet nostalgic grief can be brought me greater understanding for what Magnolia was going through. And on that note, I'd like to give my first acknowledgement to Grammy. I wish you were able to see this one too.

This book is an amalgamation of a lot of love in my life. I did, later, go back in and change the way that the loss of Iris worked in the story based on how it worked within my family. The way that Iris died is very similar to a death we crossed paths with in 2015. If you've read my first book *Feathers,* you probably know the one. Wherever that family is now, I wish them nothing but the deepest condolences and all the best in the future. From the very beginning, I pictured Poppy very much like my little brother Riley and another child my family fostered named Sophie. So I would not only like to dedicate this book to them, I'd like to thank them for being a part of my life. I would also like to thank Riley for bringing me Muffin, his stuffy from the fantastic TV show Bluey, to keep me company when I was typesetting the book.

Forever and always, I want to thank my mom. She is the absolute best and deserves the world. She is the first person I let read my manuscripts after I've finished them. I value her criticism and praise as much as I value her ridiculous comments whenever I have a very stupid typo. Forever and always, I also want to thank my dad. Not for all the times he doesn't read my posts and then asks me about them later, but for all the times he asks me what's going on in my life and I reply, "Stuff." This book is also about sisters and the unique bond between them. So, thank you, Tori for being my sister. May the three Zays bless you.

Since my last publication, I have, in fact, delivered on the pie. I no longer owe my cover designers Anjelica and Clover pie, but I do owe them my sincerest gratitude. Thank you to Clover for accepting this project when you had a lot going on in your life. And thank you to Anjelica for dealing with my nonsense for months. We came up with the absolute best cover in the end and we must let the light shine on that guitar.

Brenna Bailey was my editor and I loved every minute of that experience, even the pages long edit letter. I'm so glad that Instagram brought us together however many years ago that was. I couldn't imagine a better person to edit this project with me. I can't wait to work with you again. Brenna is also an author and I have had the pleasure of reading both her romance novels. Do yourself a favour and check out *A Tale of Two Florists*.

This is getting long, but I have to thank some of my friends now because I couldn't have kept sane over the last few months without them. First, thank you to Jessica for owning the cutest Bernese mountain dog. Blue made Rocket's breed an easy choice. Thank you, Sahar for having a cool maiden name and being lovely as usual. Lisa, once again, we will always have Geroy. Thank you for all the late night chats when I was freaking out about . . . innumerable things. Thank you to Karen, Jack, Rola, Keena, Sherry, Ali, Hilmi, and Bianca for your excitement and encouragement. And to Caitlin, Kris, and Lauren. We formed our Cass Fan Club during the pandemic and never looked back. Thank you for your support when I came to the group chat and told you that I was publishing a book this year. You guys are the best.

For anyone who bought and reviewed *Feathers*, thank you immensely. Your support brought me here. For anyone I didn't mention but played a role, somehow, I didn't forget you, I just wrote an acknowledgements way too long for a second book.

Finally, this is quite unrelated to this book in particular, but very much on my mind and in my heart. Thank you to both Kelley Armstrong and Melissa Marr for making me feel like I belonged and that my writing was worth it. That week in the highlands is something I will cherish forever.

About The Author

Madeline Nixon has been a dog walker, a nanny, a baker, a shoe saleswoman, a chocolatier, and an editor, but the title she's most fond of is author. She's published one nonfiction short story collection about her paranormal experiences, entitled *Feathers*, and several educational children's books. *Emergency Lullabies* is her debut romance novel. When she's not writing, you can find her hunting ghosts, planning elaborate theme parties, and baking whatever recipe looks the best on Pinterest. She lives in a suburb outside of Toronto.

Connect With Me!

www.madelinenixon.com

Facebook: www.facebook.com/MarkedWithAnM
Instagram: @MarkedWithAnM
Threads: @MarkedWithAnM
TikTok: @MarkedWithAnM
Twitter/X: @MarkedWithAnM

Subscribe to my newsletter
www.madelinenixon.substack.com

Don't forget to leave a review on Amazon, Goodreads, or The Storygraph!

Manufactured by Amazon.ca
Bolton, ON

35347407R00159